'I expect you long to go through women like my father does.'

'No.' Sam didn't even need to think about the question. 'You know I don't, Cathie. You're the only woman I want.'

But instead of any similar declaration herself—not, he told himself, that he'd been expecting that, although it wouldn't have been unwelcome—she merely wrinkled her nose at him again.

'Don't go serious on me again, Sam,' she said brightly. 'What's for pudding?'

'You don't get any,' he growled, wishing, briefly, that he could resist her. Even for a short time. But he couldn't. 'I get you.'

A New Zealand doctor with restless feet, **Helen Shelton** has lived and worked in Britain and travelled widely. Married to an Australian she met while on Safari in Africa, she recently moved to Sydney, where they plan to settle for a little while at least. She has always been an enthusiastic reader and writer, and inspiration for the background for her Medical Romances™ comes directly from her own experiences working in hospitals in several countries around the world.

Recent titles by the same author:

IDYLLIC INTERLUDE
A TIMELY AFFAIR
A SURGEON FOR SUSAN

COURTING CATHIE

BY
HELEN SHELTON

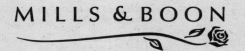

MILLS & BOON

First published in Great Britain 2000
Harlequin Mills & Boon Limited,
Eton House, 18-24 Paradise Road, Richmond, Surrey TW9 1SR

© Poppytech Services Pty, Ltd 2000

ISBN 0 263 82236 2

Set in Times Roman 10½ on 11½ pt.
03-0005-55377

Printed and bound in Spain
by Litografia Rosés, S.A., Barcelona

CHAPTER ONE

'HE'S so big,' Sam marvelled. Cradling his friends' new baby in his arms, he bounced him against his chest, grinning at the curious surprise in the infant's wide, blue-eyed gaze as he looked up at him. 'This little man's going to be an All Black when he grows up,' he declared. 'Feel the weight of him!'

'He's only average size.' Will might have been bemused by Sam's declaration about his baby son's size, but he seemed enthusiastic about his career predictions. 'He could be a rugby player, though. He's got good thighs.'

Maggie, too, seemed startled by Sam's pronouncement on her baby's size. 'Sam, what do you mean, ''big''? He's seven pounds.'

'Sam's been looking after scrawny neonates too long,' Will decreed, and Sam inclined his head, allowing that might be true. Seven pounds for a baby under his care in New Zealand's capital city's specialist neonatal unit would be considered relatively huge.

'This is probably the first time in years that you've picked up a normal newborn,' the new mother added, smiling at him. 'Now give him here,' she ordered, holding out her arms. 'We didn't invite you here to insult our new baby.'

'You didn't invite me at all,' Sam pointed out, giving up his charge with a reluctant smile. 'I had to push my way past that dragon of a midwife, two ward clerks and an SHO to get a look in here. So how are you?' Despite only eight hours having elapsed since she'd given birth, Maggie looked ravishing. Her heightened colour and sparkling pride suited her.

'Sore.' She smiled. 'But happy.'

'Ready to come back to work yet?'

She laughed. 'You wish.'

'Finding it a strain?' Will asked cheerfully.

'I'll get by.' Sam grinned. With Maggie presently planning to be off work for at least six months, and Will on paternity leave and holidays for the first eight weeks of that, he'd agreed to take on the temporary role of Director of Kapiti Hospital's intensive care unit. It was a job normally held by Will, with Maggie working as his second in command.

After two years of working in Wellington in neonates, Sam was looking forward to reacquainting himself with adult medicine again. 'It's just going to take me a few days to get used to doing my calculations in kilos instead of grams,' he added.

'Poor Sam, and they'll all be watching you,' Maggie warned, her smile suggesting she found the thought entertaining. 'Nothing gets by those nurses up there. They'll be waiting for your first mistake. Slip up and prescribe one little baby thing to one of our adults and we'll hear about it.'

'He'll keep them charmed.' Will slanted him a sideways grin. 'I hear your arrival has caused a bit of a flurry up there.'

'Today I've had one proposal, two indecent propositions and one semi-decent one,' Sam revealed. 'Is that a flurry, or just a normal day for the unit?'

'Normal day,' Will remarked dismissively, although his grin widened at his wife's affronted yelp. 'Hey, Maggie, I might be exaggerating a bit but you know what the nurses are like up there.'

'It's only meant in fun,' Sam added, laughing himself now.

'They won't all be joking,' Maggie warned mock-sternly. 'Some of them are deadly serious. Watch out.'

Sam saw the baby's tongue coming out and clearly Maggie had noticed, too, because she began unfastening her nightie in preparation for feeding him.

Sam stood. 'I should be getting back to work.'

'Stay there.' Maggie seemed amused by his haste. 'Sit. Please. I don't mind. Unless I'm embarrassing you.'

'Of course you're not.' He didn't find anything embarrassing about watching a mother feeding her child—he'd merely thought she and Will might prefer privacy. But, reassured that they were comfortable with him being there, he sat again, watching entranced as the baby fastened onto Maggie's breast. 'He's amazing,' he said softly, exchanging a brief look of mutual wonder with Will. The baby's cheeks trembled as he sucked at Maggie. 'I'm too used to seeing the unit's newborn babies being tube-fed. It seems incredible that he can feed so soon.'

'Doesn't it?' She looked up from where the baby lay happily against her. 'Before you arrived we were saying exactly the same thing ourselves. We were both expecting it to be difficult but he seemed to know what to do straight away.'

'Instinct,' he said softly, 'in action.' The baby's movement fascinated him. 'He's like a miracle. Does it hurt?'

'A little. Sort of. It's like a prickling.'

'The midwife says it won't be as bad once the milk starts to flow properly,' Will added quickly, coming to sit beside his wife. 'You know we feel totally ignorant about all of this. No one would guess we were doctors.'

'It's always different when it's happening to you or your family,' Sam agreed. 'When Dad had his heart attack last winter two cardiologists in Auckland spent half an hour debating the pros and cons of bypass surgery or angioplasty for me. Poor Dad was lying there, waiting for me to tell him what to do. I couldn't seem to take a thing in. For all I could think rationally about then, I might just as well have tossed a coin. In the end I had to tell his doctors to make the decision themselves.'

'How is your father these days?' Maggie asked.

'Good.' Sam nodded. 'Mmm. Good. We had a rough few weeks there but he's back on the farm now. Mum's given up trying to keep him resting. Last week he was out hauling hay so he must be feeling pretty fit.'

'I'm glad.' She reached out with her free hand and touched his arm. 'I like your father. You two are very alike.'

He sent her a quizzical look. 'Is that a roundabout way of calling me stubborn?'

'No other explanation for you still living in your hovel in Newtown,' Will pointed out. 'Not when we've offered you one of the best pieces of real estate in Wellington.'

Sam rolled his eyes. Since moving up to the beaches to be closer to the new hospital, Will and Maggie had been renting out their previous home in Kelburn, one of Wellington's leafiest suburbs, to a doctor working at the region's main hospital in Wellington city. Their tenant was on the verge of moving out and for the past six months they'd been trying to persuade Sam to buy the house from them. 'It's not a hovel,' he protested, defending his own Newtown home.

'It wouldn't be if you renovated,' Will agreed. 'But when are you ever going to get the time to do that?'

'When you two come back to work,' he said easily.

'You'd be better off buying the house. There's nothing to do to it. You could move in on the Saturday and have us over for a barbecue on the Sunday.'

'Maybe if you offered it at a reasonable price—'

'Sam, that price is extraordinarily reasonable,' Maggie protested laughingly. 'We all know that the view alone is worth that much. The only reason we're discounting it so massively is because it's so special to us that we want someone we love to live there.'

'On the open market it'd sell in a week,' Will declared. 'No, harbour views like that, make it a day. An hour.'

'It's perfect for you,' Maggie added. 'And Cathie likes it, doesn't she?'

'Given how little time we spend together these days, what Cathie likes or doesn't like hardly comes into the equation,' Sam countered, regretting both the words and what he suspected had been the exasperated underlying tone of his voice the instant he saw Maggie's concerned expression.

'Sorry,' he added abruptly. 'Forget that. What I meant to say was, I'll…think about it.' He managed a grin. 'Thanks. It probably is a good deal only I don't know if it's the right time to be making that sort of decision yet.'

But Maggie was still frowning. 'Sam, if there's anything we can do—'

'Cathie and I are fine.' Sam checked his watch. 'She's been working long hours lately, that's all. She's had a lot of things on. I've hardly seen her in weeks. The frustration of trying to pin her down is obviously getting to me. Look, I'd better make a move. When I left ICU there was some query about Casualty referring an admission. I should check what's going on. Congratulations, you two.' He stroked one finger lightly over the now-dozing baby's cheek. 'He's wonderful.'

The two of them exchanged unreadable looks then Maggie said tentatively, 'Wonderful enough for you to agree to be his godfather?'

'Of course.' Sam took in a deep breath, stunned by the

offer. 'I'm…speechless. Yes. Yes. I'd love that. It'd be an honour.' He kissed her cheek. 'Thank you.'

'We were going to ask Cathie if she'd be godmother,' she said hesitantly.

'I'm sure she'll be thrilled,' Sam said quickly, keeping his expression neutral. He suspected he'd have to remind Cathie about the baby having been born but he thought she would be pleased about being asked to be godmother. She was very fond of both Maggie and Will, and even if Cathie was a career type of woman at present, more than a baby one, she liked children. 'Truly. Do ask her.'

'If you're sure.'

He saw her doubts but brushed them away with a murmur about needing to get back to work. 'How long do you think you'll be staying in?'

'Home tomorrow. How about you two come for dinner Saturday night?'

'I'll get back to you on that.' He lifted his hand in a wave. 'See how you're feeling towards the end of the week. You might find you're more tired than you expect. I'll drop in tomorrow and see how you're doing.'

The unit's new admission was just arriving when he got back to the ward. 'Thirty-eight-year-old deliberate carbon monoxide poisoning,' his registrar told him quietly, coming to meet him while the nurses organised the bed. 'Tania Robinson. No loss of consciousness. Found by her husband this morning when he came home from work unexpectedly to collect something, so exposure may not have been prolonged. The neighbours don't think the car's engine was running much more than ten minutes.'

'Carboxyhaemoglobin?' Sam requested, meaning the amount of haemoglobin in her blood which had bound with the carbon monoxide rather than the oxygen it normally carried.

'Twenty-four per cent,' Phillipa told him. She handed

him the results of the test. 'She's had ten minutes of forty per cent oxygen in the ambulance and I've got her on a hundred per cent now.'

He nodded, noting the face mask and reservoir bag. 'Husband on his way?'

'He's distraught,' the other doctor told him quietly. 'A social worker's talking with him now in Casualty. He'll send him up when he thinks he can take it.'

'Pregnancy test?'

'Negative.' She smiled at his expression. 'Thought you might ask that, given your background.'

'Well done.' High carbon monoxide levels were especially lethal in pregnancy because the baby's blood took up the gas even more eagerly than the mother's blood did, meaning a baby would be at grave risk of dying or sustaining permanent damage from lack of oxygen. Pregnancy was an indication for immediate transfer to a centre with access to a chamber where hyperbaric, or high pressure, oxygen could be administered.

He went with Phillipa towards the bed. 'Mrs Robinson, I'm Sam Wheatley,' he explained. 'Dr Sam Wheatley.' He spelled it back to her and had her repeat the name to make sure she'd understood him. 'I'm one of the consultants working on the intensive care unit here. Do you have any questions for any of us?'

Above her oxygen mask, his patient closed her eyes. 'My head is aching.'

'We're organising something for that now,' he told her. 'Can you tell me where you are, Mrs Robinson?'

'The hospital.'

He noted again the slurring of her voice. 'Can you tell me the date?'

When she came back with the correct date, he nodded. 'Good.' Her nurse had her connected to the monitors now and the digital readout told him that her pulse and blood pressure were within normal limits and that her cardiac rhythm appeared normal and stable.

'A few moments ago I told you my name, Mrs Robinson.' He put his hand over the badge clipped to the lapel of his ICU gown. 'Can you remember what it was?'

'Doctor,' she said vaguely, sagging back into the pillow one of the nurses had prepared for her. 'Doctor something.'

Her heart and breath sounds were fine. He found her reflexes slightly brisker than normal but her co-ordination was reasonable and when he used an ophthalmoscope to look inside her eyes the margins of her optic discs were as clear as they should have been.

'I thought normal,' Phillipa, beside him, said quietly.

'Agreed,' he confirmed. Blurring of the discs would have been a sign of brain swelling, a common complication of carbon monoxide poisoning. 'Mrs Robinson, you're going to be with us at least a day here, depending on your blood tests.' He saw that the comment barely provoked a flicker of her lashes. 'If you have any questions, please, don't hesitate to ask.'

'When she's a bit more with it I'll do a formal suicide-risk assessment,' Phillipa told him as they drew away from the bedside. 'I've a call out for the duty psych team to come and see her. Oh, this looks like her husband arriving.'

Sam nodded. He went to greet the pale, tearful man who was pulling on a cotton gown just inside the entrance to the unit. 'Your wife's going to be all right,' he told him firmly, after introducing himself and explaining his findings and how they were treating his wife. 'There's a possibility she may have problems in the future—memory loss, for instance, and co-ordination problems—but hopefully her exposure to the carbon monoxide this morning was short enough to minimise the risk of that.'

'Thank God.' The man sagged into the chair in the small

office where Sam had taken him. 'I had no idea—' He broke off. 'Why would she do this?'

'Has she seemed depressed?'

'Worried, I suppose,' he conceded, 'about losing the baby. But I didn't realise she thought things were this bad.'

'When did she lose her baby?'

'Six months ago,' the other man said raggedly. 'We've been trying for years and she got pregnant just after we started making enquiries about fertility treatment. But after two months she began bleeding and it turned out to be a miscarriage. It's been a strain but we've started trying for another baby again. I know she's been upset but I thought she was starting to get over some of the pain now.'

'Could she have known you'd interrupt her this morning?'

'No.' He shook his head firmly and Sam saw that his hands were shaking. 'She couldn't possibly have known. I'd left a file on the porch last night when I got home when I was hurrying to get out of the rain. Even if she'd seen it there she wouldn't have known how important it was. Usually she'd have just stuck it inside where I could pick it up that night. She wouldn't have known I'd come back for it. That's what's so hard to understand, you see. She must have meant to go the whole way.'

'Phillipa Casey, the doctor you saw earlier, is arranging for a psychiatrist to come and see your wife,' Sam told him. 'I expect he or she will want to talk through things with you, too. In the meantime, we'll do everything we can medically to bring her back to full health.'

'Thank you.' The other man pushed the heel of his hand through his hair, clearly distracted. 'Can I see her?'

'Of course.' Sam opened the door for him. 'You'll find her a little vague,' he warned. 'Her short-term memory's not functioning very well at the moment but don't be frightened by that. As the oxygen clears the poison, her mind will start clearing.'

One of the senior house officers newly appointed to the unit came over to Sam as he was writing up his examination findings in their new patient's notes. 'Dr Wheatley, we were always taught that carbon monoxide poisoning turned the skin bright red,' the younger doctor said, 'but, if anything, Mrs Robinson's colour's pale.'

'The classic description is cherry red,' Sam confirmed, 'but I've never seen it in anyone who's made it into hospital alive.'

'Will she be all right?'

'Good chance.' Sam drew a quick graph and added the curve showing the difference between carbon monoxide and oxygen levels at different concentrations in the blood and demonstrated the physiology. 'Her concentrations are low enough now to suggest that with a few more hours of oxygen they'll come down fairly quickly.'

Once Phillipa had sorted out the remainder of their new patient's admission they started their evening round of their patients.

The unit had twelve beds. Ten adult beds were arranged in a wide U-shape around a central monitoring station and there were two beds in side rooms off the main part of the unit. The side-room beds could be adapted for children or, because they were on independent air-filtration systems, for patients with low immunity or potentially infectious diseases who needed to be isolated from the rest of the unit.

They could take babies and neonates in emergencies, although those needing only medium levels of care were generally looked after in the special care baby unit in the hospital's obstetric block. Those needing intensive care were usually transferred to the region's main neonatal unit in Wellington and they only kept them at Kapiti when Wellington was full.

Now, in midsummer, the unit was operating with four empty beds. In winter, with the cooler season's associated respiratory illnesses, Will had told him that they invariably ran at full capacity.

After the round they had coffee in the small staffroom attached to the unit, and he mentioned he'd been up to the postnatal ward to see the baby.

'Wasn't he tiny?' Tim, the unit's charge nurse, looked excited. 'I peeked into the ward this morning. Will was there, waiting for Maggie to wake up. Isn't he just the tiniest thing you've ever seen?'

Sam smiled, acknowledging then that his own bias definitely must be the result of his years in neonates.

'And his hair was so dark,' Tim added. 'I was expecting it to be red like Maggie's.'

'He's got Will's colouring,' Phillipa chipped in, revealing that she, too, had made the trek across to the maternity unit. 'Was the labour very long?'

'Fourteen hours,' Tim said smartly, before Sam could say anything. 'Maggie wanted a natural delivery but she had to have a shot of pethidine towards the end.'

'No gruesome details please,' Phillipa said abruptly, with a shudder. 'The thought of the pain makes me faint.'

'Phillipa,' Sam chided, smiling at that. Since he'd only been working on the unit two days, he didn't know the younger doctor well, but from her waist-length ringlets, woven head band and hippy, sixties-style of dressing, he'd have assumed she was the sort of woman to whom childbearing would come naturally. 'I thought you were an earth mother.'

'In every way but the pain,' the younger doctor confirmed with a smile. 'Remember I'm a doctor. My week in the labour ward as a student has left me permanently traumatised. Terry's been talking about wanting to have a baby soon but I told him to wait a few years. When the concept of a painless labour's perfected, I'll be in there first in line.'

'I can't imagine what makes women go through with it,' Tim said sagely. 'Jill and I are going to start trying for children soon but if it was me having to go through all that pain, I think I'd be saying, best adopt.'

'But, since it's not you, you're probably just saying, yippee, more sex,' Phillipa quipped, laughing.

'Of course I am.' Tim grinned. 'I'm not stupid. What man in his right mind is going to turn down more sex?'

Not him, Sam thought heavily, although he contained his outward reaction to a wry exchange of smiles with the other man. No, he wouldn't willingly turn down sex, he knew. At least not presently. Not when he hadn't seen Cathie in almost a month.

Sex between them had always been good. He wondered if that wasn't part of their problem. In the light of her elusiveness lately he'd started to consider whether they hadn't, until now, put too much emphasis on the sex, at the expense of maturing the less physical facets of their relationship. He was certain now that he wanted more from Cathie than regular, if spectacular sex and occasional outings. And today the memory of the way he'd felt holding Will's baby was forcing him to acknowledge just how much he wanted his own children. And how much he wanted them with Cathie.

But she wasn't going to make it easy for him. At their last meeting—he was uneasily aware that she'd been avoiding him ever since—he'd tried to talk about his discontent at the continuing casualness of their relationship, but her guarded response had made it obvious that she didn't yet share his desire for commitment.

And now, after almost four weeks without her in his bed,

he was—pathetically, he recognised with a grimace—reduced to simply craving her again. Immediately and urgently. In whatever capacity she was prepared to offer herself.

CHAPTER TWO

SAM made another determined effort to try and get hold of
Cathie before leaving the hospital, only the colleague who
answered her office telephone—his only choice as her
home machine refused to let him leave a message and since
her mobile seemed to have been switched off for at least
the last two weeks—said that she'd already left.

'She might be at the gym,' the man said offhandedly
when Sam, frustrated, pressed him. 'I think she had her
gear with her. Or she could be swimming. She never says
much but you know Cathie.'

Sam sighed. He did know Cathie. That was the problem.
'Thanks,' he said curtly, adding when the other man questioned him again about leaving one, 'No message. I left
two yesterday.'

It took him just over an hour to drive back down the
coast and into Wellington and then through town into
Newtown in the peak-hour traffic. He had given Cathie a
key to the house but it would have been unusual for her to
call in without checking with him first and, predictably, the
house was deserted.

He tried her home number again, but her machine was
still on and behaving badly. Unfastening his tie and the
buttons of his shirt as he went, he headed to his bedroom,
changed into sports clothes and headed out.

She wasn't at the gym and the receptionist at the desk
couldn't remember if she'd been in, but he saw on the
board that a pump class, one of the aerobics classes using
weights which Cathie liked, had finished twenty minutes
earlier so if she had been there he knew she'd have already

left. Driving directly to the pool, he parked the car outside, paid for his ticket, then walked through to where he could check the water.

He spied her swim cap—bright pink and distinctively adorned with the logo of the pharmaceutical company she worked for—not where she normally swam within the lanes marked off for dedicated lap swimming but in the free swimming area on the far side of the pool.

But when he came out he realised that the area he'd assumed was for free swimming had been marked off, too, that evening, and he saw that rather than simply swimming herself she was taking a class.

A qualified swimming instructor, Cathie often worked as a volunteer at the pool. In school-holiday time she taught children's classes mainly but the company she worked for was involved with a charity which helped disadvantaged adolescents and through that scheme at other times she taught teenagers.

She lifted herself out of the pool now and started marching quickly back and forth along the side, the whistle she wore on a card around her neck bouncing against the high neck of her black swimsuit as she shouted encouragement to her charges who had started swimming slowly and painstakingly up towards the shallower end of the pool.

Sam sat back against one of the rails on the lap-swimming side of the pool and watched her. She was too preoccupied with her students to be aware of him and he could have filled in the time until the end of her class by swimming laps himself, but it felt like a precious luxury to be able to be there and simply look at her.

He'd wanted Cathie from the first moment he'd seen her yet he knew that many of his friends had been surprised when they'd started dating seriously. Not that his friends didn't like her, because they invariably did, it was simply that they wouldn't have expected Sam to be with her. He understood that. In the past the women he'd tended to be attracted to had been pretty, flirtatious and fun-loving, women with whom he could spend light hours without ever worrying that there was any agenda to their involvement other than mutual enjoyment.

Cathie wasn't like that. There was no arguing with her beauty—with bewitching green eyes so darkly fringed as to be like smudges in her pale face, a generous, achingly desirable mouth, dark hair that slipped like silk between her fingers and a toned, athletic body, she seemed to him utterly beautiful.

But on the surface she was also calm and serious—intense, perhaps, sometimes even driven when it came to her career and charity work—and far too self-contained to have anything in common with his previous girlfriends. She didn't flirt, except secretly, with him, when she could drive him mad with it, and she didn't play games.

They'd met when he'd walked in late on a meeting she'd been taking. She'd flashed him a cool, irritated green look from beneath those dark lashes, but instead of feeling suitably rebuked he'd found himself spellbound and immediately aroused.

Her eyes had jerked away from him. Fast. But not before he'd registered the startled intake of breath and widening of her pupils that told him she'd experienced, just for a second, at least some faint fraction of that same chemistry.

It hadn't been love at first sight. At least not love as he understood it now. Love had grown as he'd come to know her. The passion which had flared between them meant they'd bypassed the normal, civilised getting-to-know-each other phase, meaning that instead of being put off by her seriousness and self-containment he'd instead discovered her humour and laughter and daring, as well as the strong sense of morality plus the emotional vulnerability which bubbled just beneath the calm surface of her personality.

He knew that time might eventually take the edge off the physical chemistry between them but, having fallen in love with her, he knew he'd never stop wanting her. For now, though, he still enjoyed the passion. One look, one thought, was still all it took to arouse him, and the intense, devastating magic of entering her each time, feeling her body tightening around him, remained as powerfully moving as it had that very first night.

Cathie had stopped dashing about shouting now and was hovering almost anxiously at the end of her pool as her charges neared her. Sam smiled, guessing from the excitement he could feel radiating from her despite her tense expression that this must be the first time any of them had managed to make it to a full length.

His impression was confirmed when the first hand touched the end and Cathie started clapping wildly. But when she crouched and stretched her arms out to help haul the first two swimmers out of the pool, he understood why she seemed so openly and unguardedly enthusiastic.

Her pupils weren't the children she normally coached during the school holidays but young women. Women with Down's syndrome, Sam realised, surveying each of their triumphant, beaming faces as Cathie helped them out.

'Well done,' he heard her cry above the happy shrill of her whistle being blown by one of the first women who'd climbed out. 'I'm so proud of you. Well done.'

Obviously the swim had been a big milestone for the group because a couple of the pool's regular lifeguards joined in the congratulations and celebrations, grinning widely themselves. Sam, not wanting to interrupt, waited until the pupils began dispersing towards the changing rooms before standing up.

However, before he could reach Cathie, she finished waving everyone off, adjusted her cap to include a few strands of dark hair which had worked their way loose around her ears, then executed a perfect dive from the far side of the pool and swum under to join the lap swimmers on his side.

He let her do three fast lengths, waiting until she performed an elegant turn at his end before diving in himself and following her up the pool.

At the end, before she turned, he grabbed her ankle, and when she spun around in the water and glared at him he moved closer. 'Duck under,' he ordered, indicating the swimmers in the next three lanes. 'These guys take these lanes seriously.'

'They take them seriously because they are serious,' she said evenly when they surfaced on the other side of the pool. 'Hello. What are you doing here?'

'Looking for you.' He kissed her nose. 'I saw you teaching.'

She tilted her head. 'I didn't notice you.'

'You were like a mother hen, watching your charges.'

'Oh, Sam, weren't they fantastic? You just saw the last of three hard weeks of lessons. In the beginning only one of them could even float. Can you believe that? In New Zealand! We managed to get the company to sponsor the transport and the lessons and now we're working on getting a permanent lease on a van so that it's available for trips and regular swimming for the girls from now on.'

'So this is where you've been every night these past three weeks?'

'For a couple of hours most weeknights,' she said lightly. 'But there's been a lot on at work as well. I've been going back each night after finishing here. Have you been trying to reach me?'

'About fifty times,' he groaned, pulling her into his arms. 'New suit.'

'Bought it yesterday,' she whispered. 'My old one was falling apart from the chlorine. I've missed you, too.'

'Liar.' He kissed her forehead. The non-lap part of the pool was almost empty now that her class had left as most of the other swimmers at this time were dedicated trainers, but there were still one or two observers bobbing about, meaning he wasn't about to risk their embrace growing more intimate. 'You've been too busy to miss me. You never answer the phone in your office, you haven't returned a single message and you've had your mobile switched off.'

'I've called you, too,' she protested, frowning at his disbelieving look. 'I have. This week. So don't tell *me* off for *you* not being available. You never answer your bleeper and you're never home.'

'I've been doing a one in three on call, including the last two nights. And at the weekend I was on call in town. Of course I answer my bleeper. Which hospital are you calling?'

'Wellington. Oh. Ah.' He saw her dawning comprehension. 'You're out at Kapiti this week.'

'This two months for Will,' he confirmed. 'And then another couple of months for part of Maggie's leave.'

She made a face. 'I forgot.'

'You forget anything not connected to your work.'

'I got top sales last month.'

He kissed her cheek. 'You get top sales every month.'

'Top, top sales last month. Top in the country.'

'Well done. Let's go somewhere—' she'd wrapped her legs around his beneath the water and he decided it was time they got out '—and celebrate.'

'Sam, I'd love that.' She did at least look regretful, he acknowledged, his heart sinking as he guessed what was to come. 'But I just have to work tonight,' she added quickly. 'I have to catch up on my background reading. I've got a big breakfast session tomorrow for some registrars at the hospital.'

'I'll brief you.' Cathie's initial training was in nursing

but, unhappy with both the career prospects and the financial restraints in the health service which she believed prevented her from being able to perform her job as thoroughly as she felt she ought to do, she'd diversified into pharmaceutical sales. Her job involved meeting doctors and allied health professionals and briefing them about medical advancements and her company's products. 'What field?'

'Psychiatry,' she said lightly.

'About which I know nothing,' he said heavily. It had been a good idea but one which wasn't going to work out. 'Can't you spare me a few hours?'

'Not a minute,' she said gingerly. 'At least not now. I could come by later.'

'How much later?'

She smiled. 'Around eleven?'

'That sounds good.' He slid his hands to her hips. 'Bedtime.'

'Mmm.' With her hands on his shoulders she bounced him down and kissed his mouth. 'Yummy. I'll bring my clothes for the morning. Only now I really have to dash. Sorry.'

He came with her to the edge of the pool, then lifted one hand ruefully in response to the cheerful wave she sent him before she dashed away towards the women's changing rooms. He was pathetic, he acknowledged with a groan. He knew he was merely grasping at the straws of her company as she deigned to throw them to him, but he couldn't stop himself. He wanted her too much.

It was an experience he neither liked nor—before Cathie—had ever been used to. Until her he'd only known what it had been like to be the less-involved partner in any relationship. Similar to the way he'd recognised that he'd dated women of a similar type, it hadn't been a pattern he'd chosen deliberately, not even one he'd been aware of in the past, but his relationship with Cathie had opened his eyes to that awareness.

Half-angrily, he swam under the first two strips of lane markers and into the lane dedicated to the fastest swimmers. An hour later, his body satisfactorily weary, although his emotional tension remained heightened, he hauled himself out of the pool and headed for the showers.

Cathie knocked on his front door just after ten-thirty.

'You should use your key,' he told her as he tugged her inside. 'You don't have to knock.'

'It's in my bag somewhere.' She threw her case across the floor into his lounge. 'I couldn't be bothered looking for it.'

He pulled her forward into his arms and kissed her roughly. 'You always say that.'

'Because it's always true,' she said breathlessly. 'Mmm. Something smells nice.'

'You,' he muttered into her neck, his hands busy at the front fastening of her shirt. 'Very nice.'

'It's not me, it's curry.' Pushing him away with a light laugh, she tried to peer around him. 'There's curry here.'

'Leftovers from a take-away,' he said heavily. 'You haven't eaten?'

'Not since lunch.' She skipped past him. 'I meant to after the pool but I got caught up in my studying. How's Kapiti? Are you sick of the commute?'

'They've given me a flat for when I'm on call,' he explained, following her. 'I haven't had to commute yet. At least, not both ways. Cat, it's cold. The microwave's just there. It always comes up well.'

'Too hungry,' she said brightly, spooning the leftovers onto one of his plates. 'Mmm. You're so lazy, Sam. You could have cooked these yourself, you know.'

'Too much trouble just for me,' he said, watching her

mouth as she ate with the gusto with which she did everything in life. 'How's everything going? Heard from your mum lately?'

'Harry walked out,' she told him with a sigh. 'She's pretty upset but at least he was a decent man and he hasn't stolen anything or beaten her up or anything like that.' She shook her head. 'Not like the last two. She was tearful on the phone and I was planning to fly up and stay with her for a few days, but as soon as I started talking about her picking me up at the airport she started going on about some guy she's met through work. She said she was going to invite him to spend the weekend at the house so if I came up I'd only be in the way. I think she might be in love again already.'

Sam smiled. Cathie's mother had been married and divorced four times, and the average period for her non-marital relationships seemed to be about three months. In the two years he'd known Cathie, her mother had had at least six live-in partners. Her enthusiasm for her current partner had been on the wane for several weeks now and he wasn't surprised to hear that the relationship was over. But Sam had met Harry in Auckland at Christmas and he still felt sorry for the man. As Cathie had said, he'd seemed a decent enough sort of man, and Sam suspected he hadn't known what he'd been in for when he'd got involved with Elizabeth.

'I'm glad she's all right this time,' he said calmly. Elizabeth's break-ups tended to be fraught events, with much wailing and drama and shedding of tears. Cathie, who was far too emotionally honest and direct herself to understand that her mother's hysteria might be overstated, was invariably sucked up into the trauma. 'Having another man lined up on the sidelines must be a great comfort for her.'

'She fascinates you,' Cathie said shrewdly, her eyes narrowing on him briefly. 'At least her life does. Admit it. You're always interested in how she is.'

'There is a certain fascination, yes,' he admitted evenly. 'With all your family. Coming from a family where couples throughout history have mostly stuck together till death does them part, your parents were always going to have a certain thrilling appeal.'

'I expect you long to go through women like my father does.'

'No.' Cathie's father lagged behind his ex-wife in terms of wedding and relationship numbers only by a couple, but Sam didn't even need to think about the question. He leaned back against the doorframe behind him and folded his arms, studying her face. 'You know I don't, Cathie. You're the only woman I want.'

But instead of any similar declaration herself—not, he told himself, that he'd been expecting that, although it wouldn't have been unwelcome—she merely wrinkled her little nose at him again.

'Don't go serious on me again, Sam,' she said brightly. 'You'll give me indigestion. What's for pudding?'

'You don't get any,' he growled, wishing briefly that he could resist her. Even for a short time. But he couldn't. 'I get you.'

'Sam!' she squealed, when he swept her off her chair and up onto the table, careless of the plastic pots of curry his movement sent flying. 'You're such a caveman.'

'Only with you,' he muttered against her mouth as his hands busied themselves at her clothes, baring her to his hungry gaze. 'You make me that way.'

'I like you when you're like this,' she teased, her voice torturing his senses in the same way that her hands sliding inside his shirt tortured his skin. 'Strong and determined. You've made me all excited.'

'Good.' Intent on revealing her breasts, he spared only

the briefest time to kiss her laughing mouth again, before pushing her shirt down her arms. 'You've been exciting me for the past four weeks.'

'But I haven't even seen you.'

'That's what I mean,' he muttered, shrugging off his own shirt where she'd unbuttoned it then shedding his jeans. But when he went to tug away her track pants he discovered the ankles were too tight to get them over her running shoes and he struggled with them briefly, before sending her a frustrated glare. 'Couldn't you just once wear a skirt when you come here?'

'Skirts are for work.' However, her laughter as she bent and pushed his impatient fingers aside and unfastened her own shoes was gratifyingly breathless. 'Stop complaining.' She freed her feet and kicked the pants away then wiggled her panties down to follow them. 'This wouldn't be so much fun if it was too easy.'

'It would still be fun,' he protested hoarsely, sliding his hands beneath her bare buttocks to lift her properly against him. 'It just might save me having a heart attack one day, trying to get your clothes off.'

'You're too fit to have a heart attack,' she chided, her eyes teasing as she slid against him in a way that just about sent him out of his mind.

'Don't do that,' he growled against her scented shoulder, struggling for control. It had been too long and he wanted her too much. 'Cat—'

'It's all right.' Her soft laughter vibrated through his skin. 'I want this, too, Sam. Please.'

Afterwards he carried her upstairs, gratified by the feeling of her damp, heated skin against him. He ran her a bath but as the old enamel tub was too narrow to fit both of them in it he took a shower while she soaked.

'You're long overdue for a bigger bathroom,' she called. 'If you rip out the wall into the other bedroom it'd be a decent size. You could extend your bedroom out the back at the same time and that'd let some sun in at least.'

Sam grimaced. He'd bought the house in his first year after graduation when it had seemed like a bargain, intending to take on major renovations. Over those first years he'd periodically given some thought to what had needed to be done but the hard fact was that he'd simply never had enough time to start such a big project. Now, years down the track, he still couldn't envisage any time in the future when he would have the time.

He knew he could get builders in to do everything but there was time and organisation involved in that as well, and although their work would make the house more liveable he wasn't convinced it would necessarily make it more saleable. Most of the original housing locally was old and people buying into this and surrounding areas these days seemed to be those intent on stamping their own personalities on their homes by undertaking their own renovations.

'Unless I'm going to stay here long term I don't know if it's worth starting,' he told her. 'I might be better selling it as is when the agent can label it a renovator's delight or something similar. Perhaps I should just buy something better for myself.'

'Sell the house?' Cathie sent him a startled look. 'But you love it here.'

He shrugged. Turning the water off, he grabbed the towel he'd left slung over the shower's glass door. He blotted his hair and chest before fastening the towel around his hips. 'Will and Maggie mentioned their house again today.'

'Maggie!' She slapped a hand to her mouth, her eyes wide. 'Oh, Sam, I forgot. The baby. Has she had it?'

'Early this morning.' He smiled. 'A boy. About seven pounds. Great black head of hair. He's…well, I guess you'd say he's cute.'

'What about Maggie?'

'Fine. She looks terrific. A bit pale, but that's not abnormal.'

'Stitches?' she asked gingerly.

Sam laughed. 'That's a very womanly question,' he observed, moving in and out of the bathroom as he prepared the bed then came back to brush his teeth. 'You'll have to check that one out yourself. I didn't ask and she didn't mention any.'

'Did she sort of wince and grimace as she walked about?'

'She was in bed when I was there.'

'Poor thing.' She grimaced. 'I hope she got away without them. You hear some dreadful stories. I remember one woman when I was doing my nursing training...' Then, perhaps having interpreted his alarmed expression correctly, she trailed off with a smile. 'I'll send some flowers and a note in the morning and I'll try and get out there Friday afternoon if she's in the mood for visitors.'

'They've invited us Saturday night for dinner if you're free.'

He felt himself tense when she hesitated. 'The company's got a teamwork exercise thing scheduled for the day,' she said slowly. 'It'll probably turn out to be mountain-biking or shooting paint-balls or doing a triathlon or something similar, and those sorts of things sometimes go on a bit afterwards. It's good bonding for the whole team. The last time we all ended up staying in a restaurant till almost midnight.'

Sam sighed, but he took care to keep his expression neutral. 'So I'll let Maggie know you can't make it to dinner?'

'No, don't. I would like to see the baby. And I don't want to hurt Maggie by not seeming to be very enthusiastic about seeing him.'

Sam registered her words wearily, chiding himself for having hoped for anything more. Just because holding the baby had turned his insides disturbingly mushy, it didn't follow that Cathie would be affected the same way.

She seemed to enjoy being around children. Her swim-teaching and the fact that she gave up a week of her holidays every summer to work as a volunteer instructor at a children's camp in the Marlborough Sounds told him that much at least. But with her involvement in her career and her unwillingness to commit herself to their relationship to the degree that he wanted her to, he knew that she didn't see babies and children as necessarily as relevant to her life as he saw them to his at present.

She still seemed to be thinking. 'Saturday night would certainly be easier than trying to get away early Friday afternoon.' Her face cleared slowly. 'I'll warn work that I might have to slip out early,' she told him. 'After all, the exercise starts at eight in the morning. Leaving at six at night shouldn't look too bad. Will that be all right?'

'Six is fine,' he said evenly. He'd allow an hour for her and another hour for the drive up to the coast and tell Maggie and Will to expect them by eight.

'How is Will coping?'

'He's thrilled. The baby's surprisingly active, given how young he is. Even at this stage he's looking all about, inspecting everything with huge blue eyes. I'd say he's going to be lively.'

'You sound quite smitten.' She sent him what he supposed she considered a teasing look. 'Watch out, Sam. It might only be a short step before you'll be wanting your own next.'

Sam stilled. He'd just finished rinsing his mouth but instead of putting his brush away he merely straightened slowly and looked at her reflection in the mirror. 'Cat—'

'Don't,' she said swiftly. He saw that she'd guessed what he'd been about to say because she abruptly hauled herself out of the water and didn't look at him as she wrapped herself in one of his bath towels. 'Don't start. Please, Sam. Don't upset things.'

'I'm not trying to upset things,' he said quietly. 'I'm trying to clarify them. Cathie, if you would just talk about this—'

'I don't want to talk about it,' she said sharply. Still avoiding his level gaze, she tipped her head down and released her damp hair before she gathered it in a towel. 'Why can't we go on the way we've been until now? It's so good like this, Sam. Why do you suddenly have to take everything so seriously?'

'Perhaps because I've realised that I *feel* it seriously.' Her words demonstrated an irony he felt painfully. Cathie was supposed to be the more serious one of the two of them, yet when it came to their relationship that pattern had reversed. 'I want more than seeing you a couple of times a month when you can squeeze me into your schedule,' he said carefully. 'I want us to share more.'

'I said I'd try to make more time.'

'Yes, you did. You said that almost a month ago and that was the last time I saw you,' he pointed out, keeping his tone determinedly reasonable. 'We wouldn't have had tonight if I hadn't chased halfway over town for you. Am I misreading signals here? If I'm being particularly dense about this, Cathie, you have to tell me. I need to know that. Are you trying to tell me you don't want to go on?'

Her pallor came gratifyingly swiftly, but she made no move towards him. 'Not unless you don't. Sam, I love what we have. I love spending time with you. I'd just…prefer it if you didn't get all serious on me.'

'But what's the alternative?' He saw from the uncharacteristic discomfort in her expression and the compulsive way her fingers had curled into the fabric of her towel that his demand had disturbed her, but, desperate to understand, he pushed a little more. 'Where do you want our relationship to go?'

'I don't want things to change,' she burst out.

'They'll change regardless,' he argued. 'Everything changes. That's what life is. Neither of us can alter that.' But he couldn't resist her when she looked so worried, and against his better judgement he relented. 'Cathie, it's late. We're both tired. Let's go to bed.'

'Oh, I'd like that,' she whispered. She took his hand and led him into his bedroom. 'I'd like that very much. Sam, it's just the upheaval. It's you changing jobs and my promotion, and you seeing Maggie and Will changing with the baby. It's all unsettling. No wonder you're feeling restless and questioning things. It won't take long for things to settle down and then you'll realise you like us being the way we are. You're too independent, we're both too independent, and we both love what we have too much to want anything to change. You'll realise that in a little while and then you'll understand that I'm right to want things to stay the same.'

Burying his face in the scented hollow of her throat, content for now just to hold her, Sam let her words wash over him. For the most part he thought she had everything wrong, but lying so close to her, when briefly he could pretend to himself that he had everything he wanted, it didn't feel like the right time for an argument. But it was coming.

CHAPTER THREE

TANIA ROBINSON'S blood-test results the next morning were low. 'We've brought the oxygen down overnight,' Sam's registrar told him on their morning paper round, the round where they simply worked through all the previous day's charts and results. 'There's a bed organised on one of the medical wards when you're happy for her to be transferred.'

He nodded acknowledgement. 'What about the psychiatrists?'

'The on-call doctor had a chat with her last night and she's coming back this morning. Mrs Robinson doesn't want to go to one of their wards as a voluntary patient. The psychiatrist doesn't seem to think there're any grounds for sectioning her but she'll decide after reviewing her today.'

'We've three empty beds,' Sam observed, looking around. 'Unless we need her bed let's keep her here until we have the word on that. It'll be unsettling for her if we transfer her in the meantime.' He checked with the unit's charge nurse. 'Are you OK with that, Tim?'

'Fine.' Tim nodded. 'Good idea. Having one non-ventilated patient will take some of the load off us as well this morning because we've two students on duty. Every other patient is high-dependency at the moment.'

Mrs Robinson was the last patient they had needed to discuss, and once they folded away the notes and X-rays they moved from the office back to the unit proper.

As they started moving towards Mrs Robinson, the double doors into the unit opened and Tim pulled them up.

34

'Hold on. Here's the psychiatrist arriving now. Should we skip Tania and see her later?'

'We'll start at the next bed,' Sam said, changing course. 'That'll give the psychiatrist time to finish before we interrupt.' He glanced at the doctor approaching them, then, with a grin, he stopped. 'Leslie Skinner.'

'Sam Wheatley!' With an answering beam, the other doctor skipped towards them. 'What on earth are you doing way out here?'

'I should be asking the same of you,' Sam pointed out. Leslie had been in his class through medical school and they'd dated, casually, for a brief time as medical students. After her first year as a house officer she'd been bitten by the travel bug and had headed off to Europe and, as far as he'd known, she'd been there ever since. 'Last I heard, you were taking a job in Birmingham. When did you get back?'

'About three weeks ago,' she said eagerly. 'Actually, I was thinking of calling you this weekend to try and catch up, Sam. I'm doing a locum here. But what about you? What are you doing at Kapiti? I heard you'd been offered the new ICU consultant job in town. Don't tell me you turned it down?'

'The position doesn't start till mid-year,' he revealed. 'In the meantime, I'm covering here.' Aware of Phillipa and Tim waiting to one side through all of this, he added briskly, 'We must catch up properly. Call me.'

'I'll have a chat once I've spoken to Tania here,' Leslie agreed with a smile. 'We'll arrange something then.'

The screens were still around the bed when he finished his round, and since he was scheduled to cover one of Will's pain clinics he had to leave the unit in Phillipa's hands but he asked Tim to give Leslie his bleeper number.

When she called him an hour later they arranged to meet for lunch, and shortly after one he met her in the hospital's main canteen. 'You look terrific,' he told her sincerely while they waited in the queue for their sandwiches. 'But there's something different...'

'I've bleached my hair,' she said, with a laugh. 'I found a bundle of grey strands a few months ago and they terrified me. But thank you. You, too. Sam, it's so good to see you.'

They found a table close to the window. Because the canteen was on the third floor of the main surgical and medical wing of the hospital, they had distant views of the blue Kapiti coast and, further out, the rising hills of Kapiti Island, a wildlife sanctuary a few kilometres from shore.

Leslie gazed out with apparent contentment. 'Beautiful, isn't it? I love the coast up here. When I heard they'd finally built this hospital I was thrilled. It's half the reason I came back to New Zealand.'

'What's the other half?'

'Missing my family,' she said with a sigh. 'And I remembered how lovely Kiwi men can be and I thought I might try and find myself one. I broke up with someone I'd been living with for five years.' Her quietness then suggested that the break-up had been a painful experience. 'It seemed like a good time to come home. And what about you? Help, you're wonderful to look at, Sam. I'd forgotten how gorgeous you are. Still playing the field and breaking hearts all over the hospital?'

'Those days are long gone.' Sam, dismissing her comments about his appearance with a faintly impatient shrug of his shoulder, smiled. 'Not that I imagine I ever broke any hearts. These days I'm very definitely a one-woman man.'

'I find that very hard to believe.' She fluttered her lashes at him. 'Not you, Sam. I don't believe you could ever settle down. Don't tell me you're married?'

'Not yet, but I'm certainly not as allergic to the idea as I used to be.' He started, almost, to change the subject but, having astounded himself by hearing what he'd said, added instead, 'Unfortunately, Cathie seems determined not to take my intentions seriously.'

'Oh, I like that.' Her sudden peal of amusement drew interested glances from some nurses a few tables away. 'I really like that. That's so ironic it makes my fingers tingle. You mean you, Sam Wheatley, might just be being treated like a mere sex object?'

'Something like that,' he conceded dryly, a little unsettled by the shrewdness of her insight. 'I'm trying to bring her around but it's turning into a long struggle.'

'Have you thought that maybe she's not the right woman for you?' Pausing midway through cutting the muffin she'd chosen, Leslie gave him what he supposed could be described as an old-fashioned look. 'If you are finally ready to settle down, you know there are plenty of women who'd be more than willing.'

'I haven't noticed any.' He frowned, puzzled by her obvious amusement. 'Why is that funny?'

'Sam, look at you.' She seemed to find his blank look even more amusing. 'I mean, just look at you. You're incredible-looking, you're intelligent, terrific company, you're great—and I mean *great*—in bed, and you've just landed yourself one of the best hospital jobs in the country. Frankly, speaking as a very old friend here, I'd marry you tomorrow and so would half the women in this canteen.'

He sighed. 'Leslie, that's sweet—'

'It's not sweet, you idiot man. It's true.' She rolled her eyes in the dramatic way he remembered from years earlier. 'Honestly, men can be thick sometimes. You know what I think? I think that if this woman of yours is so stupid as not to appreciate you, you should look elsewhere. Find someone who'll give you what you want.'

'Life is never that simple,' he said evasively, wanting to divert her and regretting the absurd impulse which had made him confide in her about Cathie at all. Even if it hadn't left him feeling disloyal, the situation between them was too complicated for him to explain it properly to anyone else.

While it was true that he would marry Cathie the next day if she'd have him, and true, too, that since holding Will's and Maggie's baby he'd become overwhelmingly aware of a powerful desire to hold his own children, he knew that he only wanted those things because he wanted them with Cathie. If it weren't for her, for wanting her so much, the issue of marriage and children would probably still have been a distant one for him. He briefly brought her up to date on their mutual acquaintances before asking, 'Are you home permanently, Leslie? Or just long enough to assuage your homesickness?'

'Permanently.' Her shrewd look told him she'd noted the subject change but she made no attempt to change it back. 'There's a job coming up at the new psych acute unit at Keneparu,' she said, mentioning another of the Wellington region's hospitals, 'but there's quite a bit of locum work coming up in town and here if I don't get that one. I've decided to stay. New Zealand men make good husbands, and as I want children before my time runs out I'm going to make an effort to meet some.'

He smiled. It seemed that Leslie's forthrightness hadn't been dented by her years in the UK. 'Anyone in mind?'

'You, if you do the sensible thing about your current girlfriend,' she told him.

Sam sighed. 'Leslie—'

'I know. I know.' She laughed and he realised she'd been joking. 'Stop fretting. I can see it in your eyes. You're besotted, aren't you?'

'Hopelessly,' he confessed calmly.

'Well, I hope it works out for you.' She took a mouthful of coffee then looked up at him sharply with a frown. 'Did you say *Will's* baby before? Will Saunders?' At his nod, she pushed away her coffee and shook her head. 'Will Saunders has a baby! I don't believe it. Last I heard he was head of one of the top ICUs in London.'

'He's been back a few years now,' Sam explained. 'His homesickness fitted in with him being offered the job here.' Will had been in their year at medical school as well. 'He married an English ICU consultant who came out here to work. Maggie's lovely. You'll like her. In fact, I'm covering for Will and Maggie with my locum in the unit here. Will's taken paternity leave and holidays and Maggie's expecting to be off for six months. Their first baby was born yesterday.'

Leslie banged her fist lightly on the table. 'Both you and Will taken,' she complained jokingly. 'Damn! I knew I should have come back sooner.'

'I'll give you his number.' He tore a sheet out of the notebook he was carrying in the pocket of his white coat. 'They've moved out to the coast here.' He wrote down Will's and Maggie's number, then his own as well so she had that. 'I'm sure he'd love to catch up.'

'I'd love to see the baby,' she murmured. 'I adore babies. Oh, Sam, I forgot. Tania Robinson?'

'Mmm?'

'I've explained my findings to your registrar but I guess you want to know, too. As far as I can tell, she's been clinically depressed since losing her baby six months ago. She hasn't seen any health professionals in that time so no one's picked it up. I'll follow her and her husband myself for a few months. I don't think she's at high risk of another suicide attempt at present so I'm happy about her going to a general medical ward, although I'd rather she didn't go home today.'

'Yesterday's attempt?'

'Impulsive act brought on by getting her period,' she told him. 'She's shocked by how far she overreacted and obviously relieved that she was caught in time. She hadn't planned anything at all and the only reason she tried carbon monoxide poisoning was that on the radio that morning she'd heard about someone killing himself that way. I'm confident she's thinking rationally now. She'll be fine if she's discharged tomorrow.'

'Brought on by getting her period because…she's wanting to get pregnant?' he queried, remembering her husband's comment about her previous miscarriage.

'She desperately wants to be pregnant again,' Leslie confirmed. 'This time, discovering that she wasn't, it was just too much for her. She's very conscious of the fact that she might be running out of time. As far as I can tell, none of her previous history shows any reason for either the miscarriage or why they're having difficulty conceiving now, but I'm getting her an appointment to see one of the obs and gynae people here to review things.'

'This all sounds very efficient,' he noted dryly.

'In my professional life, Sam, I am efficient,' she countered, fluttering her lashes at him. 'Oh, damn, it's almost two.' She jumped up with a start. 'I've got a massive clinic and I'm going to be late unless I leave right now. Bye, Sam. It's been great. Let's do this again soon. I'll give you a call.'

On his way out of the canteen he was bleeped to Casualty, and when he answered the call from the telephone in the corridor the casualty officer apologised for calling him directly but said that Phillipa had been unable to come to the telephone to answer his referral.

'That's fine.' Sam brushed aside the younger doctor's concern. He was happy to take direct calls when his juniors were otherwise occupied. 'What's the problem?'

'I've a forty-year-old man who's walked into Casualty complaining of three days of leg pain, trouble walking today and shortness of breath. He isn't a smoker. I've checked his blood gases and he's in type two respiratory failure, only I haven't got a clue why. His cardiograph is normal, he doesn't have a fever and his chest X-ray looks normal. If it's a pulmonary embolus, wouldn't the ECG and chest X-ray be abnormal?'

'What are the exact results?' Sam asked, nodding when the other doctor promptly recited the values. The younger man was right about the respiratory failure, and the results suggested that the failure was severe enough to warrant the man being artificially ventilated. 'I'll be there in two minutes,' he said tightly. 'He'll need to be admitted to Intensive Care.'

Sam hadn't been to Kapiti's Casualty Department before but he knew where it was and he was there well within the two minutes he'd promised. His patient was in a side room off the main trolley-bay area, but Sam took one look at the bluish tinge to his skin and his obvious tiredness and hauled his trolley out. 'Hi, Sam Wheatley,' he told the nurse looking after him, after introducing himself to their patient. 'I'm acting ICU director at the moment. You're…?'

'Lynette,' she told him.

'Lynette, let's move to Resus. Stat. Take the other end and steer, could you? Thanks. I'm sorry, sir, we're just transferring you to another part of the department,' he added to his breathless patient. 'Do you have any relatives with you?'

'We called his wife at work,' Lynette told him. 'She's at lunch but someone's going to give her the message to call us when she gets back.'

Sam waited until he had their patient positioned at the one remaining unoccupied site within the resuscitation area before taking Lynette to one side. 'Try and get hold of the wife again,' he told her, keeping his tone low. 'See if they can send someone to look for her at lunch. She should get here fast. Is there a spirometer in the department?'

'I'll bring it back with me,' she said quickly as she moved away.

Turning back to his patient with deliberate calm, he took a few seconds to explain exactly who he was and what his role was. 'The doctor who referred you to me, Mr Williams, mentioned that you'd had some pain in your legs.'

'More numbness than pain,' his patient puffed. 'My feet have been a bit strange for a few days, but the legs have only been bad today.'

As the man spoke, Sam was examining his legs. To look at and to touch they were normal, but when he tested the strength in both feet it was obviously reduced. 'Any coughs or colds?' he asked. 'Recent bout of any tummy upset?'

'I had a touch of flu last week. Bit of a cough for a few days but…nothing like this. This feels like it's…getting worse by the minute.'

Sam finished his brief examination of the man's limbs by checking his reflexes—they'd disappeared from his ankles and knees but he still had a weak response at his elbows—then he moved up to his face. 'Screw up your eyes for me, Mr Williams. Good. Whistle. Blow out your cheeks. Smile.' In keeping with his observations, there was obvious weakness in both sides of his patient's face. 'Follow my finger with your eyes.' He moved his finger in an H shape in the air, noting the defect in the way his eyes followed the movement. 'Thanks.'

Lynette, who'd been off calling Mrs. Williams, came scooting back in as Sam was finishing examining the insides of his patient's eyes. 'Your wife's on her way in,' she told Mr Williams, exchanging a quick look with Sam. She was wheeling the machine he'd requested, one which measured breathing volumes. 'Shall I do this?'

'Connect the monitors,' he said quietly. He moved out of her way so she could attach the blood-pressure cuff and cardiac leads, and moved around the other side of the bed.

He passed his patient the flexible tube attached to the machine. 'Mr Williams, I want you to take as deep a breath as you can then blow out as much air as you can into this. I want you to empty your lungs completely. Good.' He nodded as the other man put his lips to the cardboard tube at the end. 'That's it. Keep breathing. Keep breathing. Stop only when you absolutely have to.'

He watched the feeble effort impassively, gave his patient a few minutes to recover, then checked how much he could blow out quickly to complete the test. The electronic device calculated the figures he needed and confirmed what he'd already suspected. He went to wash his hands again, before completing his examination.

'Have you passed urine yet today?'

'I don't think so,' he answered, not showing any reaction when Sam, examining his abdomen, pressed on his distended bladder. 'But, then, I haven't been drinking.'

'He's in urinary retention,' Sam told Lynette. 'We'll put a catheter in on the unit.' As a precaution against introducing bacteria from other parts of the hospital, they made an effort to perform any necessary sterile procedures on the unit itself rather than prior to admission.

'BP 180 over 100,' the nurse told him quietly, indicating the digital monitor beside the bed. 'Pulse 116.'

Sam nodded. Explaining what he was about to do, he sat Mr Williams forward and tapped out his chest, then listened to it. He did the same at the front, this time listening to the heart as well as the lungs. As he'd been expecting, air entry to both bases was much reduced.

He finished by swiftly examining Mr Williams's mouth and throat. He had extensive pooling of saliva, suggesting that his swallowing was already impaired, and when Sam asked him to swallow on command the movement was weak and uncoordinated. He managed a cough but it was very weak.

· Sam drew back, inspecting him from the end of the bed again. His examination, although thorough, had been brief, and less than ten minutes had passed since he'd first walked into Casualty, but his patient was noticeably more tired. 'How long do you think for his wife?'

'Perhaps another fifty minutes?' Lynette said doubtfully.

'She works…in Wellington,' Mr Williams added weakly.

'I'll try and wait,' Sam said quietly. But he didn't think he had a lot of time. 'Mr Williams, your symptoms resemble a condition called Guillain-Barré syndrome. Have you ever heard of it?'

'It's a virus, isn't it?' The other man sent him a relieved look. 'I have heard of it. Is it like the flu I had?'

'It isn't flu,' Sam countered, 'and it's not exactly a virus, although it can occur after a viral infection.' He leaned against the bench behind him and slowly explained what the condition meant.

'For some reason, after some infections the material that covers nerves can begin to break down. That slows the conduction of impulses along the nerves and in your case that's leading to a paralysis because the impulses aren't getting through to your muscles. It can happen very quickly. The main worrying part of the syndrome is that it affects the muscles you breathe with and that's why the doctor who saw you earlier wanted me to see you so quickly. Your blood test shows that your muscles aren't working well enough to either take in enough fresh oxygen or get rid of all the carbon dioxide from your body.'

'Is this something…like polio?'

'Not exactly, although some of the treatment is a little similar. To make sure your body keeps getting enough oxygen I'm going to have to give you enough sedation to put you to sleep so that I can connect you to a ventilator. Do you understand what a ventilator is?'

'A breathing machine,' the other man confirmed breathlessly. 'I've seen them on television.'

'We can look after you very well when you're on the machine,' Sam continued. 'The other part of the treatment involves giving you transfusions of special proteins which help fight infection. We'll start that in a few hours but you'll be sedated still so you probably won't be aware it's going on. We're also going to need to take a sample of fluid out of your spine to analyse but I'll wait until you're asleep to do that, along with a test of your muscles which we need to do. Even when you seem asleep we'll talk to you and explain everything that's happening in case you can hear us.

'Ideally, I'd like to get on with things straight away because the blood test and the breathing test you just did show that your breathing is deteriorating fast, but I'm going to try and wait until your wife arrives so that you can talk to each other before I connect you to the machine. In the meantime, though, we're going to transfer you upstairs to our intensive care unit.'

He passed Lynette the notes. 'We'll need an orderly and a full resuscitation trolley for the transfer.'

The resuscitation trolley was because he was worried that he might need to intubate and ventilate their patient during the transfer, but fortunately the move to the lifts and up to the unit proved uneventful.

Lynette delivered Mrs Williams up to the ICU just as Sam was finishing briefing Phillipa and the nursing staff on their new admission. He went to talk to her and guide her across to her husband. In Sam's experience, a common reaction with relatives coming to the unit for the first time was overwhelming alarm at the machinery surrounding their loved ones. But Lynette had clearly done a good job of preparing Mrs Williams for what she would see because, although obviously shocked at seeing her husband in the state he was in, her immediate reaction was to hurry over and take his hand.

'Five minutes,' Sam said quietly, observing the feeble effort Mr Williams was making now to breathe.

As soon as that time was up, they moved quickly. Tim guided Mrs Williams out to the relatives' room while Sam smoothly sedated him in order to connect him to the ventilator that was going to take over his breathing for him.

'He was fine yesterday,' his wife said huskily, when Tim brought her back. She made the words sound like some sort of mantra as she looked up towards Sam from where she sat on a chair by the bed. 'I mean, he said his legs were a bit funny but we thought that was from the gardening he'd been doing. Can it really strike this fast, this thing?'

At Sam's nod, she rushed on, 'But I've never heard of it.'

'In the general community it's not common,' Sam said gently. 'In hospitals we see it fairly regularly.'

'He's very strong. He still plays rugby in the winter. Just a social grade but he still takes his training seriously. He never gets sick. He had a bad cold or flu a few weeks ago but that's the first time he's been ill in years. He must be going to be all right.'

'If I'm right about the diagnosis then there's every chance he'll make a complete recovery,' Sam said carefully, nodding his thanks to the casualty nurse for her help as she indicated that she needed to leave. He swung the chair around towards the bed so that his patient's wife could sit more comfortably.

'We need to do a few tests in order to try and confirm the diagnosis and I've also asked a neurologist—that's a physician who specialises in diseases of the nervous system—for a second opinion. Unfortunately, the doctor I wanted particularly is in Wellington this afternoon and won't be able to see him until the morning. However, it may still be a while before we can be certain of the diagnosis.'

'And if it's not the thing you're thinking it is?'

'The symptoms your husband described are typical of Guillain-Barré,' Sam explained. 'I'm confident that's what this is going to turn out to be. We're running some routine screening tests to look for other things, but I think we've got the right diagnosis.'

'The nurse said that you just have to keep Daniel breathing until the disease naturally goes away.'

'Broadly speaking, that's true,' he conceded, 'although there are some things we can do to speed up that happening. One of the things I discussed with your husband is a process where we can give him a transfusion of a special protein which helps fight infection, and we'll start that today. An alternative is to exchange the liquid in his blood for fresh liquid. Depending on how he responds to the protein, we may end up doing that, too, but I'll let you know what we decide on.'

She looked startled. 'So there's a chance he'll still be like this in a week?'

'It's difficult to predict.' Sam returned her gaze steadily. Because they were going to be able to start treatment so quickly after he'd first displayed symptoms, he was optimistic about her husband's prospects of recovery, yet he felt strongly that it wasn't fair to raise false hopes about how long that might take. He'd cared for patients in the past who'd been able to be weaned off the ventilator within ten days, but there had been others who'd required many months of ventilation.

'The fact that we can start treatment so soon after he started having symptoms is very good, but recovery within a week would be very fast. It may take several weeks or even longer before we can take him off this ventilator.'

'Even longer?' She paled. 'Will I be able to talk to him?'

'You can talk to him all the time. He's only sedated at the moment so that he can tolerate the ventilator. In a few days we'll wake him a little bit more. While the breathing tube is in he won't be able to talk, but unless his paralysis becomes total, and certainly after he starts to recover a little, he should be able to communicate at least by blinking.'

He heard sounds of a trolley being wheeled towards them then Prue Little, one of the senior staff nurses in the unit, appeared around the screens. 'Mrs Williams, I'm Prue,' she said with a smile. 'I'm going to be looking after Daniel this afternoon.' The pair exchanged greetings then Prue raised her brows at Sam. 'I've got an LP set ready outside,' she told him. 'Will you do that now or would you rather Tim and I did the catheter first?'

'LP,' Sam told her. They'd already positioned Mr Williams on his side for the lumbar puncture and it made sense to do it first. He explained to Mrs Williams about needing to take a sample of her husband's spinal fluid. 'It just involves numbing the skin and popping a tiny needle into his back. I won't take very long.'

He saw the grip she had on her husband's limp hand tighten. 'Can I stay?'

'Of course.' Sam had no objections if she wanted to be there.

'And what's this catheter you're talking about?'

'A bladder catheter. To drain your husband's urine. The nerves supplying his bladder muscles have been affected by the illness as well, meaning he can't pass urine normally.'

'What about food? He can't not eat and drink for a week.'

'In a little while I'm going to pop a thin tube down through his nose into his stomach,' Prue said quickly. 'We can pump water and liquid food down the tube to keep him well nourished and hydrated.'

'So much,' Mrs Williams said weakly.

'It's all part of looking after him while he can't look after himself,' Sam told her. 'Apart from the ventilator, the most important thing we can give your husband is good nursing care.'

'It just seems so strange.' She was shaking her head. 'Yesterday he was well.'

Sam left Prue to comfort her while he went to scrub for the lumbar puncture. After three years of working in neonates, with the precise skills such small-scale work demanded, it felt very strange to anaesthetise then aim his needle at an adult-sized spine. He found the correct space immediately and, before removing any fluid, he checked the pressure by measuring how high it rose within a clear manometer. When the fluid stopped rising, moving gently up and down only with each breath by the ventilator, he checked the level then let the sample he wanted drip away into his collecting vials. Then he smoothly withdrew his needle and covered the spot with the sterile dressing Prue had ready for him.

'We'll have a result on these from the lab within an hour,' he told Mrs Williams. 'They won't be able to tell us for sure about the diagnosis, but we should get a good indication.'

'A neurology technician's on her way out from town,' Phillipa told him when he returned to the unit's main desk with his samples. 'Having fun?'

'I feel like I need to get my hand in again with adults,' Sam admitted with a smile, explaining why he'd done the LP himself rather than delegating the task to Phillipa or their SHO. 'After three years of babies it felt a bit like sticking a fence spike into a weather balloon. Is the technician based here or Wellington?'

'They cover both sites,' Phillipa explained. 'She's been

in Wellington this afternoon but she's happy to come out now.'

'We need the information,' Sam confirmed, taking the sticky label she offered him from Mr Williams's notes to fix to the top of the request form he was completing. The neurology technician would be able to tell them how well the nerves supplying their patient's muscles were working. If their responses were slowed and the sample of fluid he'd taken from his spine showed signs of inflammation, the combination of results was considered fairly specific confirmation of a diagnosis of Guillain-Barré.

He put his labelled vials into a bag, along with four forms for the different laboratories which would contribute to the analysis of the fluid, then asked their ward clerk to bleep an orderly to collect them.

'I spoke to Leslie Skinner,' he told Phillipa, remembering the psychiatrist's advice. 'She said she was happy to follow up Mrs Robinson's admission.'

'We've transferred her to Kirk Ward,' Phillipa told him, referring to one of the block's general medical wards. 'The medical team's going to keep an eye on her overnight. Oh, and Will called back.' Sam had left a message earlier with Maggie on the postnatal ward. 'He said eight o'clock is fine for dinner on Saturday night.'

'Thanks.' Sam nodded. It was Thursday now so he made a mental note to confirm the timing for the evening with Cathie the next day. If she got so caught up with her company's activities on Saturday that she forgot they'd arranged to meet, it wouldn't be the first time such a thing had happened. Only this time, instead of him sitting at home or at some bar or restaurant alone waiting for her, his friends would be inconvenienced as well.

The recollections of all the evenings he'd spent alone, waiting for Cathie, were neither comfortable nor pleasant ones and he grimaced. Much as he still wanted Cathie, he reflected, at some point soon if she wouldn't give just a little bit there was going to come a time when he'd have to decide how much longer his pride could handle her.

CHAPTER FOUR

SAM wasn't able to get hold of Cathie at work the next day, forcing him, finally, to leave a message with one of her colleagues confirming the timing for Saturday, so he was still half-surprised when someone knocked on his door shortly after seven the next evening.

'Look at your face,' she said accusingly, when he opened the door. 'You thought I'd forgotten.'

'It wouldn't be the first time,' he pointed out reasonably, but he smiled. 'Hi. Come in.' Since she seemed so intent on not doing it, he decided to give up suggesting she use her key. 'You look wonderful.'

'I feel exhausted,' she told him, brushing her heels on his porch mat before she came inside. 'They blindfolded us, took our money away and drove us way around the harbour past Eastbourne along some track out to Pencarrow Heads, and made us find our way back. Hi.' She kissed him. 'You smell nice. Love the shirt.'

'I have great taste,' he told her evenly when she sent him a meaningful look. Both the linen shirt he was wearing and his aftershave had been presents from her for his last birthday. 'How did you get out?'

'Canny Martin had a feeling something like that was going to happen,' she explained. 'He'd taped an ATM card to his stomach. It took us less than an hour to tramp out and then he just got a cash advance and we had lunch out there then got a bus back into town.'

'So why are you exhausted?'

'Martin and I took our bikes out around the bays. We had a strong head wind all the way back.'

52

'You should have called me. I wouldn't have minded a ride.'

'You were on call last night. I thought you'd be working.'

'Only till this morning.' He'd handed over to the anaesthetist who was covering ICU for the weekend that morning and had been back in town by lunchtime. 'Do I know this Martin?'

'He's a new rep.' She laughed. 'Don't narrow your eyes at me like that, Sam. He's nice enough but he's not in your league. He doesn't make my legs weak.'

'Is that what I do?'

'You know very well you do,' she said, kissing him again. 'More than my legs when you kiss me like that. You always have. Right from that first day you walked into that awful meeting. Mmm. Nice.' She lifted her silky shirt and drew his hand to one bare breast. 'Do we have time?'

'None,' he admitted huskily. Bending his head, he slid his tongue briefly across one tightened nipple, before drawing away from her with a reluctant groan to check his watch. 'They're expecting us by eight.' He let her shirt fall to cover her. 'We'd better move.'

Traffic was fairly light and from his house it was a relatively short drive to the start of the motorway, which then took them soaring along the city's downtown high-rise business district and briefly around the harbour, before heading up into the hills. 'Did I really turn your legs weak that first day?'

'Of course you did,' she said lightly. 'I just about fell over.' He felt her amused gaze prickle at the side of his face. 'You must have noticed. From the moment you walked in my speech went out the window. I'd prepared dozens of overhead projection things but I forgot completely to show them. In fact, I wouldn't be surprised if I spoke nothing but gibberish the rest of the hour.'

'It sounded all right to me.' Aside from a vague recollection that her presentation had concerned new drug developments in paediatric intensive care, he couldn't recall much of that first talk. He'd been far too preoccupied by her effect on him to take much notice of what she'd been saying. But on every occasion when he'd heard her speak professionally since—even when the heated flash of her eyes in his direction had told him that she was as aware of him as he was of her—he'd found her confident, controlled and professional delivery enormously impressive. 'And you were annoyed at me being late.'

'I wasn't annoyed, I was swooning.' She laughed. 'Sam, you know what you did to me. You know exactly. I could hardly think. You walked in, looked me up and down and my stomach did a back flip. I'd been warned about you but I still had no defence.'

'Warned?' He spared her a quick frown. 'What are you talking about?'

'Laura Elves.'

'Laura Elves?' Sam winced. 'Ah.'

'Ah, yourself.'

'You've kept that little surprise hidden a long time.'

'We used to nurse together,' she said lightly, but he registered her lack of denial about having kept that information deliberately from him. 'Years ago in Casualty. I didn't know her that well and I haven't seen her since she moved to Auckland, but when I got the job covering the hospital in Wellington she did tell me quite a lot about her ex-boyfriend, Dr Sam Wheatley.'

'Cathie…' Sam took in a breath, but then stopped, contemplating how best to proceed. 'Laura and I weren't—'

'She doesn't bear any grudges, Sam.' She stroked his thigh in a way he assumed she'd meant to be reassuring, although in reality he found her touch almost unbearably arousing. 'She only wanted me to know that you were a terrible flirt and that if you ever turned those devastating blue eyes in my direction I shouldn't make the same mistake as she did and take you too seriously.'

'I'm hardly a flirt—' he began impatiently, only she didn't let him finish.

'Sam, you used to be.'

He groaned. 'Perhaps as a student—'

'But you were qualified long before you and Laura started going out.'

'Laura and I never went out,' he protested. 'At least, not the way she seemed to think we were going out. We had a few jokes on the ward from time to time and, yes, we had a couple of dates—'

'You went to bed with her.'

He sighed. 'I don't recall any objection from her at the time.'

'Oh, I'm sure she didn't object.' Laughing, she put her small hand on his thigh again. 'On the contrary, knowing you, I'm sure she had a wonderful time. It's all right, Sam. None of this is any of my business. You don't have to explain anything to me.'

But he wanted to. The thought that Laura might have given her a biased view of their brief relationship bothered him. 'I made a mistake with Laura,' he said heavily. 'I didn't deliberately mislead her but I didn't realise how serious she was.'

He'd worked with the nurse for about three months and he'd taken her to the movies and out to dinner a couple of times, but when she'd invited him along to a family barbecue he'd had no idea how much she'd read into what for him had been a purely casual interest.

When he'd gone into her parents' kitchen to deposit the wine he'd brought, he'd spied a cake decorated with his and Laura's names and two rings enclosed within a huge pink heart. His own heart sinking, he'd gone outside and from then on it had been appallingly obvious that both she and her family were fully expecting him to use the occasion to make his intentions—intentions he didn't have—known and propose to Laura. Somehow he'd managed to get through the afternoon and make his escape before dessert time, and the next day he'd taken care to explain to her that his interest was in friendship, not marriage. But for months afterwards, until she'd changed jobs, he'd had to put up with a deluge of hurt, soulful looks from her. 'I thought she understood—'

'That you have as much interest in marriage as you do in rearing chickens,' she finished cheerfully. 'I think poor Laura got the message in the end.'

Sam sent her a sideways look. 'Well, you know I've been giving a lot of thought to chicken-rearing lately.'

'Don't, Sam.' Until then the mood inside the car had been buoyant but now it tightened and he sensed her become tense. 'Let's not argue. Not now.'

'We don't have to argue.' Pulling out smoothly to overtake an empty sheep truck, he took care to keep his tone light. 'We never have to argue. In fact, we never have to argue again ever. You just have to learn to say, "Yes, Sam. Of course, Sam. Whatever you say, Sam."'

'Three bags full, Sam.' He must have got something right with either his tone or his words because the air lightened again. 'Oh, no, that wouldn't do at all,' she said cheerfully. 'You're far too sure of yourself already.'

Considering the way he felt around her, Sam found the irony of her words exquisite, but he didn't say anything until a short while later when he turned into Maggie's and Will's driveway. 'Why didn't the things that Laura told you make you wary of me?' Captivated, he'd invited Cathie out after the meeting that first day and they'd ended up in his bed that night. 'Why didn't you tell me to get lost?'

'What?' She seemed astounded by the question. 'Sam,

be reasonable. Just you looking at me made me want to take my clothes off. I'd never felt anything like that before. Never. Not remotely. The only man I'd ever…' She faltered a little, her voice breaking softly, and although he tensed himself for some revelation about her previous relationships, a subject she'd always avoided before, she veered away from the subject. 'Well, suffice it to say that I'd never understood what it meant to be thoroughly aroused before.'

She took a deep breath, and when he didn't say anything she rushed on, 'Sam, I know this must sound immoral, and part of me hates myself for knowing it, but it wouldn't have mattered to me that night if you hadn't also wanted me. I would have pursued you shamelessly. I'd have chased you and pestered you until you couldn't fight me any longer. Dinner that night was a complete waste of time. I've tried to think, since, where it was that we went, but I don't remember. All I know is that I spent the whole night trying to stop myself dragging you out of the restaurant and back to your car. I wanted you so much it hurt.'

'Cat, you know I felt the same.' He touched her cheek, her throat, then let his finger trail to the corner of her mouth, then down to the breast he ached to see uncovered again. 'I wanted you just as much.'

'It's still like that for me,' she said tightly. She pressed her breast into his palm and he felt its small hardened crest lifting against him. 'I still catch fire when you look at me. Nothing's changed.'

'We have to go in.' It came out like a groan. He longed to uncover her, to kiss the nub of flesh against his palm and soothe her, but he could hardly make love to her in Maggie's and Will's driveway. He took his hand away and readjusted her shirt. 'Later, hmm?'

'This dinner,' she declared unevenly, 'is going to seem rather long.'

Will answered the door to them and drew them into the main living area. 'We've ordered Thai,' Maggie said apologetically in a rush, coming forward to greet them. 'From a restaurant around the corner. I hope you don't mind. We meant to cook but we've been so busy and we still really wanted to see you both—'

'Thai's terrific,' Sam said evenly, bending to kiss her soft cheek. 'We both love Thai. And we were both a bit surprised you thought you were up to having us over so quickly.'

'Neither of us realised how much work there'd be,' Will contributed wryly. 'He doesn't seem to sleep much. We've only had a couple of hours ourselves since we brought him home.'

'You poor things.' Cathie, beside him, was smiling. 'You both look wonderful but I suppose underneath you must be exhausted.'

'The exhilaration's still there, covering it up,' Maggie said softly. 'Do you want to see him?'

'Oh, yes.' Cathie went after her towards what Sam assumed was the nursery and he couldn't resist following them. 'Have you decided on a name yet?'

'We've narrowed it down to Richard James, James Richard or Timothy Richard James,' Maggie whispered, rolling her eyes. 'Richard is Will's father's name and James was my father's, but neither of us like Dick or Jim if they're shortened. We don't mind Tim, though, and since there are Timothys in both our families we're beginning to think it might be a neutral alternative. We're still thinking. Oh, I can't believe it.' They all peered over the cot. 'Just when we want him wide awake he's finally asleep.'

'He's beautiful,' Cathie whispered back, and Sam, watching her, felt himself gripped inside by some sort of edgy excitement as he saw how her face softened. 'But he's so little.'

'Tell Sam that.' Maggie smiled at him. 'He thinks he's a monster.'

'Sam's out of touch with reality.' Cathie sent him a teasing look. 'He used to make me celebrate with him every time one of his tiniest babies got to five hundred grams.'

'Any excuse for a party,' he murmured, squeezing her hand. 'You'll have to come and see him again when he's awake. He's got huge blue eyes you could drown in.' The way I feel as if I could drown in yours, he added silently, still holding her hand. 'He'll probably be up all night now.'

'Don't even joke about it,' Will said wryly. 'We definitely don't need another night like the last one.'

'They settle down pretty quickly,' Cathie said confidently. When they all, including Sam, looked at her doubtfully she added, a little less confidently, 'Well, at least, I've heard some parents say they do.'

'Fingers crossed,' Maggie added strongly. 'I thought a baby was going to be a breeze after years of a one in three on call. It never occurred to me that it could be more tiring.'

The chime of the doorbell interrupted them and Sam, thinking he could help with the take-aways, followed Will out of the nursery to answer it. Only, as well as the man with their food, Leslie was just coming towards the door, and as Will kissed her enthusiastically and ushered her in he explained that Leslie had called him that morning and he'd invited her along.

Soon after that Maggie and Cathie came out from the nursery and Sam, always aware of Cathie, stilled as he sensed tension in the faint stiffness of her expression, a stiffness matched, he thought, somehow in Maggie's face, too. He sent Cathie a questioning look but she avoided his gaze, and if he'd been right about any awkwardness between the two women it seemed to dissolve quickly in the flurry of introductions demanded by the new arrival.

'Leslie, Sam, Jerry and I all shared this awful old hospital flat when we were fourth-year medical students,' Will explained to Maggie and Cathie. 'By Jerry I mean Jeremy Donaldson, the medical superintendent at Kapiti,' he added for Cathie's benefit. 'We had a great year together.'

'I see your cooking skills haven't improved,' Leslie quipped, eyeing the trays of food Will and Sam still bore.

'He's not too bad,' Maggie said lightly. 'I'm sorry, Leslie. I know it's rude to invite people and not cook. We meant to do something—'

'Take no notice of me, Maggie. I'm sorry. I'm just being rude to Will, I didn't mean anything by it. And I'm joking.' Leslie flapped her hand in the air. 'I love Thai. Also anyone who invites people for dinner, take-away or whatever, three days after giving birth has my awed and total admiration,' she added smoothly. 'Speaking of babies, I'm dying to see this one. As the years tick by I'm finding myself unbearably clucky. Is he awake?'

'I'll show you anyway,' Maggie said, looking pleased. 'He's just through here.'

While the two women were occupied, he and Cathie helped Will set out the food. 'Cathie...?' Sam touched her chin when they were alone briefly while Will went off to hunt out wine and beers. 'Are you all right?'

'Of course.' But her smile looked slightly forced. 'Why wouldn't I be?'

Dinner went well, largely, he thought, because of Leslie whose happy chatter overrode Cathie's strained quietness. Not that her silence was obvious to anyone but him, he suspected, because Cathie wasn't the sort to chatter herself. It was just that he was, as always, exquisitely sensitive to her.

Leslie seemed to have a never-ending supply of anecdotes from the year they'd all lived together, and she kept the conversation bubbling and sparkling and there were many smiles and much laughter.

Cathie, he thought, despite her quietness, seemed entertained by Leslie's tales. Towards the end of the meal, though, he surprised a certain pensiveness in her expression when she surveyed him, but that quickly changed to something private and far more heated when she realised that he was watching her back.

Tearing his gaze away, he saw that Maggie was starting to suppress yawns and he made movements towards a quick departure. 'No arguments,' he said firmly, when Maggie seemed about to deny her tiredness. 'We're close enough friends to not need to be polite about things like this. You should grab sleep when you can.'

Before leaving, they looked in on the baby again, and since he was awake Sam held him and cooed at him for a few minutes. Cathie backed away, shaking her head, when he offered him to her, murmuring something he didn't hear but which was obviously negative so he passed the infant to Leslie and they made their farewells.

'Sam, don't let's go back yet.' Cathie put her hand on his thigh as he turned right at the first intersection. 'Not yet. Take me to the beach.'

He drove until they found a secluded stretch of sand where the road curved away. 'This makes me feel like I'm a student again,' he said hoarsely when she moved to come over him. He slid his seat back as far as it could go. He loved her like this. He loved the wild, careless creature she could turn into in their secret moments. 'Wouldn't you rather have a comfortable bed?'

'Too far away.' Already bare from the waist down, she lifted herself against him with a husky laugh. 'Stop fighting me. What's happened to your sense of adventure?'

'I think it died when I turned thirty,' he said hoarsely, but her movements were distracting him from his anxiety at the unorthodox venue. 'You're crazy.'

'Not crazy.' Her hair fell across his face. 'Just impatient. Don't stop.'

There was a cool wind blowing across the beach and stirring up the sand later when they climbed out of the car, but Cathie just laughed at him when he protested, and her laughter taunted him into discarding his clothes alongside hers on the sand and following her into the inky waves.

'You see, it's not so bad,' she teased, swimming into his arms and tucking her legs over his thighs, her hands twined around his neck so they bobbed together. 'It's lovely when you're in.'

'It's public,' he pointed out mildly, casting a wary look back towards the beach and the car park. The cloud covering the moon above them was thick enough to mean they'd be concealed if another car should arrive at that moment, but there was no guarantee it would stay like that. 'Is it the danger of getting caught that turns you on?'

'Not the danger,' she countered lightly. 'It's you.' She opened her mouth over his. 'Mmm. Good. More.'

On the drive back towards Wellington an hour later she told him that she didn't need to do any work the next day. 'I'm yours for the whole day if you're interested.'

'You know I'm interested.' He'd always be interested. 'We could walk around the bays and see if the penguins are there.'

'I'd like that.' She went quiet for a little but then she reached over and turned down the Brahms CD they'd been listening to, as if she wanted to talk. 'Leslie seemed nice.'

'She is.' He sent her a quizzical look. They were approaching the hospital now, and in the orange glow filtering into the car from the lights outside the car her expression was unreadable. 'She's a lot of fun.'

'I can tell that.'

He reversed into the space behind Cathie's sedan outside his house.

'Does it bother you to talk about her?' she asked softly.

'No.' But when she didn't ask anything else he didn't volunteer any information.

Inside the house, she discarded her damp clothes as soon as she got inside the door, sending him a cheeky look before marching naked with them towards his laundry. 'You'd better undress,' she called. 'The salt will leave stains.' He heard his washing machine being opened. 'If you've ruined these pants I'm going to make you pay for a new pair. You should have let me come home naked, the way I wanted.'

'We'd definitely have been stopped by the police then,' he chided. They'd been waved through two drink-driving checkpoints on the way back to the city. 'I stopped you from being arrested.'

She laughed. 'I'd have charmed them.'

'Oh, you'd have charmed them all right.' Following her into the laundry with his clothes, he dumped them into the machine then cupped her silky breasts. 'At least, these would have charmed them, but you'd still have been arrested. You'd have been all over the papers in the morning, bare as the day you were born, and I'd have had all my friends ringing me up, telling me how lucky I am.'

'I think I'd like to try a comfortable bed now,' she whispered.

'My pleasure.' He switched on the machine then scooped her up and carried her upstairs and tumbled her onto it.

Later they lay collapsed together spoon-fashion, her bottom warm against him, her breast cupped in his palm and pale in the clear moonlight which filtered into the bedroom through the slats in the timber blinds.

'Leslie seemed nice,' she murmured.

Sam frowned. He pressed his mouth gently to her neck. 'I thought we'd already had this conversation.' Their sweat-dampened bodies were melded so closely together he couldn't avoid feeling her stiffen.

'I thought we didn't finish it.'

'What's to finish?'

With a soft sound she wiggled free of him and turned onto her side to face him, stretching herself so that her head rested on one long, extended arm while she watched him, her eyes dark and huge in her pale face. 'Were you properly involved?'

'Properly involved?' Puzzled as much by her words as by the direction her questions were taking, he eased himself onto his back, supporting his head on his bent arm on the pillow. 'Properly involved,' he mused. 'Are you asking if we slept together?'

'Sam, it's blindingly obvious you slept together,' she said evenly, and he saw she smiled a little at his startled look. 'Come on, I'm not stupid. The way she looks at you would have told me that even if her stories hadn't. You don't need to tell me anything about the sex. It's none of my business. Neither is this, but I'm still curious. What I meant was, were you *emotionally* involved?'

He rolled onto his side to study her properly, unable to resist drifting his hand along the soft curve between her waist and her hips. 'You're talking about a long time ago.'

'So the answer's yes?'

'No. No, it isn't.' He didn't feel especially comfortable discussing Leslie, but as it was so rare for Cathie to show any sort of interest in his previous relationships and given that it was the second time that evening she'd demonstrated any such interest, he was curious to know where it would lead. 'We flatted together for a year and were friends all that time. But we didn't...go out until after that. It was exam time and we were both under a bit of stress and...it seemed like a way of relaxing, I suppose. It was very low key. I doubt even Will knows about it.'

'Were you in love with her?'

'No.' He answered immediately, but then hesitated, hoping that he hadn't sounded too unfeeling. 'I was fond of her,' he added slowly. 'We had fun. It wasn't just sex, but it wasn't anything particularly intense either. Not on either side.'

'So how did it end?'

'It died out.' He leaned back into the pillows, closing his eyes. 'And then she left. We were near the beginning of our trainee intern year,' he explained. The trainee internship was the combined study and working year New Zealand doctors did between final written exams and starting as house officers full time in hospitals. 'For family reasons she'd applied to swap from Wellington to Christchurch and her transfer came through. We were both pretty busy and gradually we lost touch. A few years later she went to England and she's been there ever since.'

'And tonight's the first time you've seen her since?'

'We had lunch one day this week,' he said. 'I gave her Will's number. That's how she came to be invited tonight.' He kissed her shoulder. 'Any more questions or is the inquisition over?'

'She's very attractive.'

He smoothed her hair out of the way and moved his mouth to the side of her throat. 'I prefer sexy brunettes.'

'She still wants you.'

He laughed. 'You're imagining it.'

'I'm not, you know.'

'Are you jealous?'

'Not jealous,' she said softly. 'Curious, perhaps.'

'About the past?'

'About…you.' But instead of clarifying anything about that cryptic little remark, she simply wriggled a little, settling herself against him. 'Wake me early,' she said softly. 'We should leave early for our walk.'

In the morning they bought buns at Sam's local baker and drove down to one of the bays where they walked around the rocks to have a breakfast picnic in the area where seals and sometimes penguins were found.

The last time they'd made the trek there'd been a small group of penguins, as well as lots of seals, but today there were just bare, sea-drenched rocks. 'Autumn's the best time,' Cathie said. 'There are always dozens here in autumn.'

They continued around the coast, dawdling over some of the rock pools scattered along the wild, rocky shore. 'I'm starving,' he protested, as lunchtime came and went. 'We should have brought more food. Let's go back.'

'Lazy.' Cathie, who was crouched beside a pool, teasing a tiny sea anemone with her little finger, scooped up water with her palm and splashed him with it. 'Just another hour. We could easily make it up the hill to Brooklyn from here.'

'And then what?' he questioned dryly. They'd be miles from where they'd left his car. 'How will we get back?'

'It's not too far to my place from there to walk.'

'Ha.'

'We could hitchhike.'

'No, thanks.'

'It'll be fun,' she insisted lightly.

'I'm too old for that sort of fun. Come on.' Too hungry to let her argue the point, he scooped her up, ignoring her squealing protests as he carried her back towards the track. 'Where've you left your shoes?'

'On the grass.' Laughing, she pointed towards a patch on the other side of the beach. 'Over there. You like it when I let you boss me about, don't you?'

'Mmm.' He smiled. She was right. 'I like it a lot.' He knelt and put her down onto the grassy sand, then lifted her small feet onto his jeans-clad thighs and brushed the bottoms of them free of damp sand. 'If you don't get it all off they'll rub inside your shoes. Why in the world can't you wear socks, like a normal person?'

'I don't like them making my feet hot.'

'They don't make your feet hot.' The argument exasperated him just as much now as it had done the first time he'd heard her use it two years before. 'If anything, they do the opposite and they protect your feet, especially when your shoes are new like these ones.' He brushed her left heel where it had become reddened and a little puffy. 'See? You're getting a blister. This is going to hurt like mad later.'

But instead of looking, she simply lay back on her elbows, her expression playful, her green eyes sparkling. 'Kiss it better for me?'

He pressed a chaste kiss to the salt-scented edge of her heel, then tickled her when she wiggled her foot at him as if to demand more. 'You're too sandy.'

'My lips aren't sandy,' she protested.

Smiling, he leaned forward and tasted them, then tasted again and once more to be sure. 'Sunscreen,' he pronounced finally. He'd seen her earlier, applying the stick. 'Factor fifteen.'

'Twenty-five,' she declared softly. She put her hand around the back of his head and brought him back down atop her, spreading her thighs so that he lay between them. 'It's so nice here,' she murmured. 'In the grass. With the waves. Let's rest a while. I feel sleepy.'

'You're not sleepy.' Sam knew her expressions better than he knew his own, and the mischievous green glow in her eyes wasn't sleepiness. 'Cat, this thing you're getting for sex in public places is getting out of hand. It's broad daylight. We're only just off the path.'

'There's no one around,' she argued reasonably, peppering his chin with tiny kisses. 'We haven't seen a soul for ages. Or are you telling me you're too old for this sort of fun as well suddenly?'

'Not too old.' The heavy thudding of his pulse told him that much at least. 'Perhaps not enough of an exhibitionist.'

'No one will see.' Laughing at him, she wriggled free of her jeans and panties and kicked them away, then lowered her fingers to his own fastenings. 'Let me undo you. Just these. Come on. It won't take long. Hurry, Sam, or someone might come.'

'That's what I'm worried about,' he protested with a groan, but he knew he wasn't fooling either of them. Parting her shirt with shaking hands to give his mouth access to her breasts, he gave in to her soft pleas and buried himself in her.

They walked back slowly afterwards, stopping here and there to catch each other in languid kisses so that it took far longer to get back to the car than it had taken to get there in the beginning. He drove to Island Bay and they bought hot meat pies and milkshakes from a dairy near the beach and ate them, sitting cross-legged in the warm sand.

'We should have brought our togs,' Cathie said dreamily, lying back in the sand once she'd finished her lunch. The beach wasn't busy but there were a few families at the other end and a couple of bobbing heads out in the surf. 'I'm too lazy to run back and fetch them.'

'Don't look at me like that,' he said lazily, amused by her mock-innocent gaze. He took off his hat and pulled his sunglasses down to cover his eyes then swung around to rest his head on her stomach. 'I'm not driving all the way back just for you. You had a swim last night.'

'But the water looks so wonderful.'

'If you're that desperate, pretend your underwear's a bikini.'

'It'd have to be a topless bikini.' He felt her hands in his hair and their slow rhythmic movement as she massaged his scalp was almost hypnotic. 'I'm not wearing a bra.'

He smiled, contemplating that. 'Tired?'

'A bit.' He felt the sudden movement of her abdomen beneath his head as she yawned. 'Not surprising since you kept me awake most of the night. I might just close my eyes for a few minutes.'

That sounded good to him. Sam settled himself deeper into a comfortable position, yawning himself now as he felt his body gently drifting off to sleep.

A touch of some sort on his face woke him, and when he opened his eyes his head was in her lap and she was smiling down at him. 'It's after six,' she said softly. 'Sleepyhead.'

'After six?' He lifted his wrist, not believing her, but she was right. 'You should have woken me.'

'I was watching you.'

'That must have been boring,' he said thickly, his voice still fuzzy from sleep.

'It wasn't boring at all.' At some stage while he'd been sleeping she must have loosened her ponytail because when she brought her head down and kissed him, soft, gleaming strands of hair fell around him, tickling his cheeks and throat. 'In fact, you're very compelling. You are quite incredibly beautiful, Sam. Only usually you're awake before me and I don't get the chance to look at you properly.'

'Not so compelling that you always do what I want you to do,' he pointed out quietly.

'Perhaps not.'

He regretted his words almost as soon as he'd voiced them because her expression had stiffened. 'But, then, that *would* be boring, wouldn't it?' she said tightly. 'We should be going.'

'Yes.' He lifted his head to free her, then came up onto his heels and held out his hand to help her. 'How's the blister?'

'There isn't a blister.' But she hopped about a little, looking. 'Well, perhaps just a little one.'

'Show me.' Positioning his body to support her, he lifted her foot to inspect it himself, but to his surprise she was right. There was a blister but it was very small and it didn't look too angry. 'You were lucky this time,' he pronounced, 'but if you'd worn socks you wouldn't even have had a problem.'

'Only horribly hot feet,' she mumbled, skipping ahead of him when he lightly slapped her wiggling bottom. Once they were inside his car, her hand on his arm stilled him as he went to start it. 'Thank you for a wonderful day, Sam.'

'Thank you back,' he said softly, frowning a little at her own frown. 'It's been wonderful because you've been here and it's not over yet. What's up?'

'Nothing.' A quick shake of her head sent her hair swishing against her face.

'Are you staying for dinner?' he asked as he started the car. 'Have you got enough clothes to stay tonight?'

'I brought stuff for the morning,' she confirmed with a nod. 'I just need to iron a shirt before work. Is that all right?'

'Of course it's all right.' He cast her a half-impatient look. She knew as well as he did that if he had his way she'd be living with him all the time instead of just on rare weekends. 'Why you're so attached to that horrible flat you're renting, I can't imagine. If I bought Will's house, would you move in?'

'Are you really thinking of buying it?' she asked quickly, and he registered immediately that hadn't answered his question. 'I heard him mention it again to you last night,' she added, 'but the way you were joking around with him about the price I didn't think you were serious.'

They were outside his house now and he waited until they were parked and out of the car to add anything more. 'We'd have more room there.'

'*You* would have more room, you mean.' She was busy clapping her running shoes over his garden to get rid of the sand in them and she didn't look up, although to him her answer had been vitally important. 'It's got nothing to do with me. I'd need to save a few more years before I could think about affording to buy into a place like that.'

'I'm not suggesting you buy into it,' he said carefully. He put his key into the front door lock, then turned back to her. 'I'm suggesting I buy it for both of us.'

CHAPTER FIVE

CATHIE straightened slowly, each fraction of a second seeming to Sam like a piece of eternity, but her expression, when he could finally see it, was so guarded it almost hurt him to look at her. 'Are you suggesting I come and live with you?'

'Cathie, we both know I've been asking that for months, just as we both know you've been very carefully ignoring me,' he said huskily. 'Now I'm asking you to marry me.'

Sure that she must have guessed that was coming, her abrupt pallor in response to his words surprised him just as much as her expression suggested he'd surprised her.

'Oh…' But instead of finishing, she sank down again, sitting this time on the lowest of the five wooden steps leading up to his house. 'Oh. I wasn't expecting that,' she said thickly.

'I don't know why not.' He thought he managed to give the wry words the right touch of lightness. His limbs working automatically, he left the door and came to sit beside her. 'It's only formalising what I've told you dozens of times. And I've been dropping enough hints. I've started to say something a few times but every time I get serious you cut me off.'

'Sam, I do love you.'

'I know you do, Cat.' He kissed the top of her head, telling himself that everything was going to be all right even though it didn't feel like that at all. 'I know that. And I love you. That's why I want us to get married. I'm sorry it wasn't a very romantic proposal.' He'd meant to get a ring and take her somewhere beautiful and go down on one

72

knee, but the time had seemed right to tell her his intentions. 'But just because it wasn't romantic doesn't mean it wasn't heartfelt. I've never felt more strongly about anything in my life.'

'It's not that, Sam.' He heard the tiny sound of her swallowing. 'It's not that it wasn't romantic. It's just that I didn't think you'd ever choose to tie yourself down to a wife.'

'I don't think marriage means being tied down,' he countered. 'Once I might have thought that, perhaps, but that was before I understood how it felt to love someone the way I love you. Marriage is a sharing thing, not a taking over. Cathie, I love you. I want to share my life with you. I want to be with you for ever. I want us to have children and grow old together. Don't you want those things?'

'Sam, it's a big step.' The face she turned to him seemed full of despair but strong as well, as if to say that there was no way he'd be able to convince her otherwise. 'Marriage…children—they're huge steps.'

'I don't mean there's any immediate hurry to have babies,' he said quietly. Cathie was seven years younger than he. He wanted children with her but biologically, he acknowledged, there was no need for any rush. 'But seeing Maggie's and Will's baby has made me realise how much I want them eventually. Being his godparents means we'll have enough contact with him to assuage my paternal feelings for a while, I suppose—'

'I'm not going to be the baby's godmother.'

'You mean Will and Maggie haven't asked you yet?' He frowned. 'I thought they were going to call you last week. I'm surprised they didn't mention it last night.'

'Maggie did,' she said stiffly. 'When you went to answer the door for the food she mentioned it to me. But I said I didn't think it was a good idea. I…I said no.'

'No?' He stared at her, stunned. 'Why on earth would you say no?'

'I said that I thought it might be awkward.'

'*Awkward?* What are you talking about?'

'I meant in the future.' She'd hung her head and her hair, irritatingly, had swung forward and it hid her expression from him. 'Sam, Will and Maggie are your friends. I'm very fond of them and I'd like to think we'll always be friends now, but if I hadn't known you I would only have known them professionally. If we broke up, both of us being godparents would be very awkward.'

'But we're not,' he pointed out carefully, 'about to break up. Cathie, I've just asked you to marry me.'

She reached out and stroked a cool hand across his cheek. 'You're very used to getting your own way,' she said softly. 'It's your work, I suppose. You're used to people following orders.'

He caught her hand and pressed his mouth to her palm and didn't let her go, but his smile felt shattered. 'You don't have to try and salvage my ego here. We both know it's a long time since I had my way in anything with you,' he said quietly. 'And I've never been brave enough to order you to do anything. You're turning me down.'

'I am, I'm sorry.' Her eyes had gone very dark and very solemn, but still a faint smile lifted the corners of her mouth when he groaned.

'Cat—'

'Don't look at me like that,' she chided. 'Like a great lost dog. You knew what I'd say.'

'I suspected it but I didn't know for sure,' he protested. 'There was always a chance I might manage to sweep you off your feet.'

'You've been sweeping me off my feet for years,' she said weakly.

'So make it permanent.'

'I can't.'

'Why are you so frightened?'

'I'm not frightened. It's just…' She trailed off, but he could see her struggling to come up with something for him. 'It's just that I don't want to lose what we have now.' She lifted one shoulder uncertainly. 'It's too precious to me, Sam. You're too precious to me. I don't want to risk that.'

He tried to understand her but he couldn't. The logic of her argument escaped him. 'Cat, we're not going to lose anything,' he said reasonably. 'Getting married isn't taking a risk. It's gaining something. It's both of us gaining something. Everything. The way I see it, taking that step and making that commitment to each other means preserving what we have.'

'How can you be sure?' she demanded helplessly. 'Neither of us can be sure of that. Marriage changes things between people.'

'For the better,' he insisted.

'If it was for the better then there wouldn't be so many divorces.'

'But that wouldn't happen to us—' He stopped, then groaned, knowing that, aside from reassurances that their love would last for eternity, he didn't really have any rational argument for her claim. 'I've fallen in love with a confirmed spinster.'

At her sudden burst of laughter he scowled. 'Don't,' he growled. 'It's not funny—it's tragic.'

But she laughed again and, despite his frustration, the sound was so infectious it drew a reluctant smile from him. 'Hoist with your own petard,' she taunted lightly. 'I'm sorry, Sam. I wish it could be different. I understand what you're thinking and I wish I could be different for you. But I can't. I love you but I can't pretend to feel any other way than I do about this. So, are you going to dump me, then?'

'Dump you?' He stared at her vaguely, his thoughts confused again. 'What are you talking about?'

'Now you've finally decided you want the works?'

'The works?'

'Marriage, children, posh house.' She waved her arm about in a curving sweep, suggesting she saw the ideas as some sort of vast separate universe beyond her understanding, but despite the lightness of her voice he saw her small face had turned serious again and her eyes were achingly large. 'You know, the works.'

'Is that why you said no to being a godmother last night? Did you think I'd boot you out when you said no to me?'

'I thought you might be starting to get a little frustrated with me,' she said huskily.

'A *little*?' Sam rolled his eyes. 'Oh, yeah. A little.'

'So, are you?'

'Hmm?'

'Booting me out?'

'I don't know.' Wanting to punish her, he regarded her through narrowed eyes. 'I might keep you around till I choose someone else more suitable.'

'I knew it.' Something in his expression must have told her he was playing with her because she promptly rolled her eyes at him then spun around and sat herself across his knees and the step, straddling him. 'Now you're clucky, any woman will do.'

'Mmm.' He let her think that. 'I think I'll try a blonde next,' he mused, wrapping his arms around her back and pulling her against him. 'You career-driven brunettes are too fickle for me.'

'Thank you for not being too cross,' she whispered.

'Oh, I'm cross,' he said evenly. He took a pretend nip at her cheek, smiling when she recoiled with a sharp shriek. 'In fact, I'm seething inside. But I'll get you, Cathie Morris.

Don't think I'm giving up. You're going to be mine in the end.'

'I'm yours already,' she murmured, lifting her hips slightly against him. 'In the important ways.'

'So forget the wedding.' He tightened his grip on her hips to hold her still. 'Since the thought terrifies you so much I suppose I can compromise on that. We don't need any licence to tell us how we feel. But move in with me. I'll buy the house in Kelburn and we can sit up there on the hill, watching the ferries coming in for the next fifty years.'

'Fifty?' She laughed. 'So there really are plans to trade me in for a younger model when I get too many wrinkles for you?'

'Give or take a decade,' he said with a shrug. 'What about it, Cat?'

'Sam, I still don't understand what's wrong with what we have now.'

'Everything's wrong with it,' he grumbled. 'I love your mouth.'

'I love your body.' She ran her tongue lightly over his lower lip and sent his pulse soaring. 'What we have is perfect. Why change perfection?'

'It's not perfection,' he countered heavily. 'I hardly see you.'

'I'll make more time.'

'How much time?'

'As much as I can.'

He groaned. 'You're driving me crazy.'

'Me, too.' Although the suggestive way she shifted against him told him that she meant the words in an entirely different way to him, he couldn't resist her when she whispered, 'Take me to bed, Sam.'

Cathie rose early the next morning because she had another presentation she wanted to do some preparation for and, his bed having lost much of its attraction once she was out of it, Sam also got up early and they breakfasted together.

'This is nice,' he observed mildly as they sat in his kitchen, munching cereal together.

'The Weetbix?'

'Breakfast together,' he countered sternly, rolling his eyes when her prompt giggle showed she'd merely been teasing him. 'It doesn't happen very often.'

'It is nice,' she said quickly. She dropped her spoon, checked her watch, then came around to kiss him in one smooth movement. 'But I have to dash.' He caught the scent of his soap on the cool skin above the neck of her blouse, but she dodged away from him when he went to kiss her there. 'Are you busy Wednesday night? I should be free. We could meet in town.'

'I'm on call.' As a consultant on call in Wellington he'd been more or less free to do what he'd wanted, when he hadn't been busy, but being on call at Kapiti meant staying out at the hospital because it was too far to drive back in an emergency. 'How about coming up to the coast and visiting me? They've given me a little town-house thing on site. You could stay.'

'I'll call you.' Dancing away from his seeking hands with a soft laugh, she evaded him. 'Bye.'

He watched her go. 'Mmm.'

Because of his early start he got out to the hospital by seven. He'd assumed it was too early for any of his juniors to be in, but to his surprise Phillipa was already on the unit.

'I was on call last night,' she reminded him, 'but by the looks of you I still got more sleep than you did. Are you still doing shifts in town?'

'I just had a couple of late nights,' he said evenly, lifting up a spinal X-ray, partly out of interest but partly in an attempt to distract her. 'Who's this?'

'New patient. Six o'clock last night.' She pulled out a set of scans for him to inspect. 'High-speed head-on into a power pole. Twenty-two-year-old woman. It took two hours to extricate her from the wreck. Semi-conscious throughout until she was in the ambulance when she lost consciousness. Glasgow coma score five on arrival in Casualty.'

'Spinal X-rays, head CT normal,' Sam murmured, examining each quickly in turn. 'Main problems?'

'Ruptured spleen, multiple pelvic fractures with disruption of pelvic stability.' She pushed up another two sets of X-rays for him to examine. 'Left-sided rib fractures.' She showed him the chest X-ray which showed the rib fractures as well as increased lung markings beneath them, suggesting damage to the underlying lung.

'Compound fracture right femur and compound fractures right tibia and fib. Predicted mortality on admission to the unit sixty-five per cent. The surgeons have taken out the spleen and the orthopods have done the leg and all the abrasions, and they spent six or seven hours in Theatre with her, stabilising her pelvis. We seem to be winning the battle to keep up her cardiac output and blood pressure, but her renal function's not great and her clotting's going off this morning.'

Sam took the results she passed him. They suggested a major problem with her clotting system where the clotting factors became activated in the blood, paradoxically leaving her at high risk of haemorrhaging from her injuries. With her multiple pelvic fractures she was particularly at risk of lethal bleeding from those sites. 'How much blood before this?'

'Eighteen units of fresh, three of plasma—also, Dr Davidson has given her five bags of platelets this morning and a couple of cryo.'

'Start with another six of platelets,' he told her, and when she reached for the telephone to order the clotting cells he checked through the rest of their new admission's results. Her blood-gas results were acceptable on the machine but the initial difficulty they seemed to have had with the ventilator suggested he'd been right to assume from the chest X-ray that her lung was fairly severely bruised. 'Is this the latest chest?'

Phillipa pushed another one at him. 'That's from six this morning. Not much change.'

She came with him to see their new patient, helping him close the screens around them and the bed.

Sam checked the name card above the bed. 'Good morning, Jill.' He always spoke to his patients, regardless of whether they were conscious or not. He'd been surprised too often by their recollections once they were over their illnesses and injuries not to. 'I'm Sam Wheatley. I'm another one of the doctors here.' He ran his eye over the various machines monitoring her heart and lungs and circulation, then bent to examine her, explaining carefully as he did so what he was doing.

'Have the surgeons discussed feeding?'

'Enteral to start slowly tomorrow,' Phillipa told him, meaning that they were going to start feeding via a tube into her stomach.

'Has anyone had a look down into that lung?'

'Not yet. Do you want to?'

'Straight away,' he confirmed. He wouldn't be happy until he knew exactly what he was dealing with under those rib fractures. 'I'll do that this morning. How about relatives?'

'Her parents have been in but they've gone home to sleep. I said that nothing was likely to happen very fast.'

'It's the next few days which will be the worst,' Sam agreed. Multiple organ trauma invariably signalled a stormy course ahead. Straightforward injuries like broken legs or ribs, which were fine usually in isolation, became infinitely more complicated in combination with pelvic fractures and organ trauma—particularly with the added complication of a long delay in getting to hospital. 'I'll have a chat with them when they come back.'

They opened the screen and moved out into the central area of the unit. He saw that Daniel Williams in the next bed was still being ventilated and looked sedated.

His spinal fluid results and the nerve-muscle conduction tests on Thursday afternoon had come back as consistent with a diagnosis of Guillain-Barré syndrome, the acute paralysis Sam had been expecting, and the neurologist who'd seen him on Friday had agreed with the diagnosis. On Saturday morning Sam and the consultant on call for the unit for the weekend had discussed the possibility of reducing his sedation and waking him up a little.

'Is Mr Williams still sedated?'

'We've had trouble controlling his blood pressure,' Phillipa told him as they went over to him. 'Dr Davidson thought it safer not to wake him up yet.'

Sam wasn't sure he agreed. In his experience, the cardiac features of GBS persisted despite sedation. Like the nerves affecting the muscles and causing weakness, the syndrome also affected the internal nerves that controlled bladder function, heart rate and blood pressure. It was relatively common for both blood pressure and pulse to become labile. 'What have you started?'

'Propranolol twice daily,' she told him, indicating the chart and referring to a beta-blocker drug which both reduced the pulse rate and blood pressure. 'Plus nifedipine when it's needed for pressure spikes. He's had two doses in the past twenty-four hours.'

Sam nodded, happy to leave the standard treatment in place for the time being. Lifting the morning's chart free of the ones beneath it, he ran his finger along the previous day's recordings and blood-gas results.

'I want to get in early with a tracheostomy,' he decided. 'There's every indication that he's going to need ventilation for more than just a few more days.' A tracheostomy was a small hole made through the skin of the throat into the trachea, the breathing tube. Unit policy was to use the nose or mouth only for short-term ventilation.

When patients were expected to require mechanical ventilation for more than a week the preferred method was via a tracheostomy. Neither method was risk-free but the tracheostomy tube was less likely to be dislodged accidentally and it meant that the sedation otherwise needed before patients could tolerate the ET tube could be reduced.

'I'll speak with the surgeons.' Although as an anaesthetist he was skilled at the procedure and had performed it many times before, conventional ICU protocol these days dictated that in the non-emergency situation a specialist surgeon was asked to do it. 'Is there any particular one Will prefers to use here?'

The registrar gave him two names as they moved away from the bed, and when Sam frowned his unfamiliarity with the second name she explained that the reason he didn't know the surgeon was that he was a new, full-time appointee to the hospital.

He nodded. Although being based in Wellington meant he knew most of the doctors who worked at Kapiti part time and at the city hospital the other part, he was yet to meet many of the new, full-time hospital appointees. 'No other new admissions?'

'We had one Saturday morning with an overdose but he went to the psychiatrists yesterday,' the registrar told him. 'Jill, our power-pole crash girl, was our only admission yesterday but she was complicated enough to keep me out of mischief.'

Sam spent most of the morning moving between the unit and the paperwork accumulating in his office. At lunchtime he headed down to the hospital's purpose-built day surgery unit because the week before he'd agreed to cover a theatre list for one of his colleagues who'd gone on leave for a fortnight.

Although for the previous three years he'd largely super-specialised in paediatric anaesthetics, working in both Intensive Care and Theatres to cover paediatric surgery, he'd maintained some contact with adult anaesthetics through a weekly half-day day-surgery list in Wellington so he was relaxed about the list.

He checked through each patient in turn, taking quick histories and examining their chests and mouths, as well as checking the cardiograms those over fifty-five had had to make sure there were no contraindications for day surgery.

Day-surgery anaesthetics was a relatively new area of expertise which had evolved with changes in surgical equipment and techniques and also types of anaesthesia and pain relief. Part of the aim of day-surgery anaesthesia was to minimise side effects such as nausea and drowsiness and thus allow the early discharge which patients, along with hospital accountants, seemed to demand.

'How about allergies?' he asked a forty-five-year-old woman who'd come in for an operation on a small umbilical hernia. When she shook her head firmly he ran through his routine systems review, concentrating on the areas which concerned him the most. 'Any breathlessness? Pain in your chest when you're exercising or in cold weather? Racing of the heart or thumping in your chest?'

At all of those she shook her head, although when he bent to examine her she said, 'Actually, Doctor, I do get the occasional twinge in the chest if I'm racing about. Nothing major. My son's been under a bit of stress with his university exams at the end of the year. He has to sit some special extra exams in a few weeks. I've been worried for him. I expect it's just that.'

Sam straightened. 'Tell me about the pain.'

'It's really nothing, Doctor.' But when she put up her hand to tuck a lock of hair behind her ear he saw that her hand was shaking a little. 'Just a twinge. Here, in the middle.' She put the heel of her hand over her breastbone. 'Not over my heart or anything. It doesn't go anywhere else. I'm at that time when I'm starting to get hot flushes and fainting fits so I wondered if they might be connected.'

'Are you still having your periods?'

'They're a bit scanty these days but they're still coming,' she affirmed. 'From the fainting and things, I'm expecting the change to be coming soon, though.'

He took her wrist to check her pulse. 'Do you have any breathlessness associated with this pain?'

'The odd little bit, I suppose.'

Sam frowned. Still holding her wrist, he moved his other hand to the carotid pulsation in her neck. 'How often are you getting faint or dizzy?'

'Really only two or three times.'

'In total?'

'This morning,' she said slowly. 'A couple of times last week. Perhaps once or twice before that. It is the menopause, isn't it?'

There was a blood-pressure cuff and a manometer on the wall next to her bed, and Sam used them to check the pressure in both her arms, before examining her chest. As he'd half expected from the characteristics of her pulse, her apex beat—the impulse from the base of her heart—was more prominent than usual. When he listened with his stethoscope he heard extra sounds.

He drew back slowly, wondering how best to convey urgency without alarm. 'Have you ever had rheumatic heart disease? As a child or a young adult perhaps?'

'I don't think so, Doctor.' Obviously his questions were

disturbing her. 'Is there something wrong with my heart?' she asked sharply. 'Can you hear something in there?'

'I can hear some clicking coming from one of the valves in your heart.'

'Is it serious?'

'Heart valves are a bit like valves anywhere,' he explained carefully. 'They're designed to regulate the fluid that flows through them. The heart valves open to let blood flow in and out, and close while the heart builds pressure before pumping so that the blood doesn't simply flow out backwards again. Sometimes they get damaged or sometimes they're not formed absolutely properly in the beginning. They can grow leaky or become scarred and narrow so that it becomes hard for the heart to push blood through them.

'And there's something wrong with my valves?'

'One of them sounds a bit narrowed,' he confirmed. 'If that's the case then it would help explain why you've been a bit faint. I think it's important to get on and check you out properly. I'd like a cardiologist to see you. There's a scan we can do, rather like the scan pregnant mothers have and not at all painful, where we can get some pictures of the valves and see exactly what's happening.'

'Is it serious?'

'If your valve is damaged, it may mean an operation to replace it,' he said frankly. After examining her, he had little doubt that surgery would be required. 'But even a cardiologist wouldn't be able to say for sure until you have that scan.'

'And in the meantime, what about my hernia? I've been waiting six months—'

'Best to get this sorted first,' he interrupted. If her condition was as he suspected, surgery could be lethal. 'I'm going to postpone your operation.'

She was wringing her hands. 'But I've come all this way, Doctor.'

'While you're here I'll speak to one of the cardiologists at the hospital. She may be able to do your scan today while you're here, which means your journey won't have been wasted.'

Fortunately he'd already checked out the rest of the list patients because when he emerged from the cubicle two theatre orderlies were already wheeling the first on the list away towards the theatre next door.

Given that they could hardly start without him, Sam wasn't especially worried, but fortunately the cardiologist on call for the week answered her bleeper promptly.

'Liz, it's Sam Wheatley,' he said when he answered, and they exchanged pleasantries. He'd knew the cardiologist through his work in Wellington and he had great respect for her clinical skills. 'Hi. Yes, I'm up here, covering Will's leave for the baby. Liz, I'm doing a day-surgery list downstairs and I've just seen a woman with fairly florid signs of aortic stenosis. There's no history of rheumatic fever as far as she's aware so this may be congenital but, after listening to her history and examining her, I'd say there's not a lot of time to spare here.'

'I'll be right down, Sam.' She sounded concerned. 'Do you think she needs to go into town?'

'I think there's a good chance,' he conceded. The region's specialist cardiothoracic surgery unit was based in Wellington. 'Even if it's just an admission medically for assessment. If I'm right, she's at high risk of sudden death and I'd be frightened about letting her just go home.'

'I'll be down in a few minutes.'

'I'll be in the theatre next door,' he explained. 'If I get a spare minute between cases I'll look in on you.'

When he did get a chance to get away for a few minutes between his second and third cases, he hauled on a gown to cover his theatre gear and went to the ward. He found the cardiologist writing up her notes at the main desk, having finished her examination.

'What do you think?'

'Major stenosis,' she told him, confirming his diagnosis. She'd obviously brought her ECHO machine—the machine which performed the scan he'd explained to his patient—down to the ward because she passed him a still picture of the valve. 'I'm transferring her into town this afternoon. Until now she's barely taken any notice of her symptoms. Lucky she had to come in for her hernia.'

He nodded. 'Thanks.'

'Thank *you*.' She beamed. 'You've probably saved her life, picking it up like this. I take it from this that you're coping all right with looking after big people again.'

'It's still disconcerting having to walk around beds all the time, instead of simply turning my patients around, but I'm managing.'

'Missing the babies?'

'Some,' he conceded. 'But I didn't mean to stay in paeds so long. My main interest has always been ICU.' He'd gone into paediatric anaesthetics initially because there'd been a convenient opening at a time when he'd needed a position and because he'd had considerable experience in the field as a registrar. 'How's Charlie?'

'He's been fine post-op.' Charlie Wilkins was a baby who'd been born prematurely in Sam's last week in the neonatal unit. They'd quickly discovered that the major blood vessels supplying the baby's lungs and body had developed in a swapped-around position. Sam had escorted him up to Auckland for the urgent surgery he'd needed. 'We got him back last week,' the other doctor continued. 'He's thriving.'

'Good to hear.' Sam made a note to drop into Wellington one night soon to have a look at him.

Everything seemed to be fairly in control on the unit when he got back after his list. Tim was still on duty as charge nurse—the nurses in ICU had recently shifted to twelve-hour shifts—and he came around with Sam and Phillipa for their evening round, along with the medical registrar who'd be on call for them overnight.

'His blood pressure's been more controlled this afternoon than it was overnight,' said Hine, Mr Williams's nurse, indicating the chart. 'His pulse has been fairly steady.'

Sam nodded. 'One of the ENT registrars bleeped me as I was coming up here. They can fit in his tracheostomy tomorrow morning at eight-thirty.'

'Mrs Williams said she'll be back by seven,' Hine revealed.

'If you call me when she arrives I'll go through the consent form with her,' Sam instructed.

Will had given him his office to use while he was here, and as he'd taken most of the weekend off his paperwork was building up relentlessly despite the start he'd made on it that morning. 'I'll be here late.'

On Tuesday night he stayed late as well to review a transfer he'd accepted from Wellington because the ICU at the main hospital was full. He didn't get home until ten. There was a message on his machine from Cathie, and although she said she'd call again the next day he remembered that she'd been considering coming out to Kapiti to meet him the following evening and so he called her back.

When a drowsy male voice answered he didn't think much about it—Cathie's flatmate seemed to go through boyfriends in a similar fashion to the way Cathie went through Weetbix—but Sam simply said who he was and asked for Cathie.

'Cathie's busy,' he was told thickly. 'She's soaping that delicious little body of hers in a long, hot shower. It's late and she's had a hard day and she doesn't need to be pes-

tered by late night phone calls. Call back tomorrow, man.
In business hours.'

'She'll talk to me,' Sam said strongly. 'Who the hell is
this?'

'It's Martin,' the voice came back, sounding more
animated now. 'Cathie's boyfriend. And who the hell
are you?'

CHAPTER SIX

IT TOOK Sam eleven minutes from door to door. Fifteen to twenty was what he normally allowed. He'd done it in thirteen once. But eleven was a record. Cathie opened it even before he knocked, her face flushed, her body obviously damply bare beneath her robe which looked as if it had been pulled on in a hurry. He felt his body's reaction to her even with everything he knew now, and it sickened him.

'Don't!' she said urgently, when he went to push the door open. 'Sam, don't.' She stood in his way, pushing him back when he didn't stop. 'You're overreacting. Martin was just being silly. He's had too much to drink. We went to dinner after work and he drank for hours. He didn't mean anything. I couldn't believe it when he told me what he'd said. I tried to call you but you must have left already. Sam, there's no need for this.'

'There's a need,' he said strongly. He'd never considered himself a violent man but he felt violent now. Moving her aside, he stalked inside, intent on finding Martin. 'Where is he?'

'Asleep.'

'But not down here,' he observed harshly, staring at the empty couch in the living area. There were only two bedrooms in the flat. 'With Susan?'

'Susan's got Nick staying over,' she said weakly. She caught his arm. 'Sam, listen to me—'

'I want to see.'

'There's nothing to see. He's sleeping.'

'In your bed?'

'It seemed like the best place for him.'

Sam whirled around and charged up the stairs. He heard Cathie run after him, but he knew, from the coarse snoring he could hear as he came to the top, that she had been right about Martin sleeping. He thrust her door open and glared in disgust at the man who lay sprawled, fully clothed, across her bed, his mouth open and stinking of alcohol.

'We all went out after work to celebrate our new figures and…and a few other things, and some of the others came back here afterwards. I thought Martin was coming up to use the bathroom but when he didn't come back down I realised he was asleep. By then the others had left and he was too heavy to shift. It seemed best to let him sleep it off.' Cathie spoke quietly beside him. 'Your call must have woken him. I'm not interested in him, Sam. You're mad to think I would be.'

'I'm not going to take any more of this, Cathie.' Weary now, his fury drained by seeing the pathetic creature he'd allowed to rile him so much, he put his arm around her and hugged her into his side.

'I've had enough,' he said heavily. 'I'm not going to wait months for you to make up your mind. I don't want you living in this place now.' He eyed the long, damp pieces of wallpaper curling away from the wall. 'I don't want to have to communicate with you through colleagues and secretaries. I don't want to go weeks without seeing you and I don't want you bringing drunken men home to your bed. I want you with me. Tonight. Now.'

She nestled her head into his shoulder. 'Sam, we agreed about this on Sunday.'

'*I* didn't agree anything,' he said wearily. 'I let you have your way again, and I've had enough of giving in all the time.' It was just about killing him but he felt as if he'd just had his insides wrenched out and left exposed on the footpath, and he needed them back. 'I'm sorry. I've tried to be understanding and patient but I'm at the end of the road now. On Sunday you told me you wished you could be different, but now I wish I could. But I can't. Come home with me.'

She looked up at him, her eyes huge. 'Is this an ultimatum, Sam?'

'I can live without the wedding. If you're so unsure about marriage I can accept that. For now. But I want you with me. Come home.'

'Now?' She looked around uncertainly. 'You mean you really do mean tonight?'

It astounded him that she seemed to think he'd leave her there. The man might look pathetically wretched now but that didn't mean he'd be as useless when he woke. 'Cathie—'

'He won't wake up,' she said swiftly. 'Besides, Susan and Nick are in the next room. There's no reason to be worried about me.'

'You mean you're actually planning to share the bed with him?' he demanded, horrified.

'I can't sleep on the sofa,' she protested. 'It's too lumpy. Besides, he's harmless. And it wouldn't be the first time—'

'What—?'

'Top and tail,' she said slowly. 'Perfectly innocently. Sam, we're work colleagues. I feel sorry for him, that's all. He's new here. He doesn't know anybody else and he says he doesn't find it very easy to make friends. I can understand that. He drinks too much because he's lonely. Basically he's harmless. If you could just help me roll him over so that he's square—'

'If I could just help you roll him over, like hell,' he grated, furious that she'd let sympathy for the drunken slob overcome her reserve and good sense. Sam couldn't believe she thought he'd let the man rest. He'd sooner throttle him than make it easier for him to share her bed. 'I'm going to wake the bast—'

'Don't hurt him!' she cried.

He wouldn't. At least not yet. Not when the sod was practically unconscious. But it still felt good to haul him up by his collar and throw his muttering body out of the room. 'Where do I leave him?'

She called out the street name as she came hurrying after them down the stairs. 'You have to go back down the hill and up the other side. Past the shops. I'll come with you.'

'You're not dressed.' He needed both hands to get the drunken idiot downstairs, so he couldn't wave her back. 'Pack while you're waiting for me to get back. What number?'

'Fifty-four, I think. Or maybe forty-four. It's on the downhill side with a white picket fence and a red door.'

'Wake up.' Sam's grip on Martin's collar tightened as he shoved him roughly out into the night air. 'What number?'

'Forty-six,' he gurgled, waking marginally more when he was shoved into the back seat of Sam's car. 'Hey! What? What's going on?'

Sam climbed into the driver's seat, tipped the switch that locked the car's doors, then drove off, ignoring the vague complaints emerging behind him. The house was about a ten-minute drive away. It would have been quicker to walk because there were pedestrian walkways and steps up the hill, but he didn't begrudge the drive. He just wanted to get rid of Martin.

He double-parked in the steep street, careless of the fact that he was blocking the road should anyone need to pass. Then he hauled his passenger out and bundled him up to the door. 'Keys?'

'Keys,' the man burbled, fumbling in a pocket. 'Keys.'

Sam snatched them out of his hand, unlocked the door

and pushed him inside. Tempted to leave him there, stranded against the wall in the hallway, he imagined Cathie's reaction to that, gritted his teeth and pushed the man along until he came to a bedroom.

'Bed,' he snarled, pushing him onto it. 'Blankets.' He hauled the bedding out from under him, left them draped over him and stalked out.

He was half expecting Cathie's door to be locked against him when he got back but to his relief she'd left it open. He walked slowly up to her room, his steps heavy on the carpeted stairs, steeling himself for whatever fight they had to have, but instead Cathie, dressed now, was frantically balling clothes into a backpack.

He sagged against the doorframe. 'Cat...?'

'I can't believe those two have slept through this,' she said breathlessly, nodding her head to indicate the wall her room shared with her flatmate's bedroom. 'They must be in a coma. I'll have to leave Susan a note.'

He watched her dully, still having trouble understanding what he was seeing. 'You're coming?'

'You said it was over if I didn't.'

'Yes.'

'Well, then, of course I'm coming. Those four weeks we didn't see each other were pretty hard for me, Sam. I'm not ready to go cold turkey on the sex yet.'

He started to smile, ready to see that as a joke, but instead of any trace of lightness her face was utterly calm, as if she'd meant the comment seriously. He hesitated. 'Cathie...'

'Come on, Sam.' To his relief she did at least smile then. 'Don't have second thoughts on me now. Not when I've just destroyed all my hard work, ironing, by packing this stuff so fast. You're supposed to be cheerful and triumphant.'

He waited to feel triumphant but it didn't come. He was

too tired, he decided. 'I'll take this,' he told her. The pack was full but not heavy and he swung it easily over one shoulder. 'What about your things in the wardrobe?'

'I'll bring enough for the week and get the rest at the weekend.' She swept off a row of hangers and folded them along with the clothes they held over her arm, then looked around the small room without any particular expression. 'I can't think of anything else I'm likely to need immediately.'

Neither of them said anything on the drive back to his house. He carried her pack and some of her clothes inside and she brought the rest. He swept his own clothes along to one end of his wardrobe to make room for hers.

He took a shower while she unpacked and when he came out she was already in bed. It should have felt right, he knew. It should have felt great. He had got what he wanted. Yet it didn't feel like any of those things.

He turned off the light, got into bed and gathered her warm body against him. As always, the touch of her aroused him, and the answering soft pressure of her buttocks against him suggested she felt the same, but for the first time in two years he found himself not wanting to make love, but merely to hold her.

He felt her stiffen against him as if his inactivity disturbed her, but he simply stroked her gently from shoulder to hip, again and again, loving the smooth, soft warmth of her skin, soothing her, and gradually he felt her stiffness relax and a little while later her breathing deepened and he felt her drift off to sleep in his arms.

Sam had assumed that once they were living together they'd have far more time together, but it only took a couple of weeks for him to realise that hope had been forlorn. He was seeing her more often, yes, but their total time together—outside bed—didn't seem to have changed.

Not that that was her fault, he conceded, admitting that with both Maggie and one of his anaesthetic consultants on leave, he was having to spend every third and occasionally every second night out at Kapiti covering the unit and sometimes Theatres.

But on the nights in between it seemed that the occasional evening Cathie didn't spend working late on a presentation she was scheduled to give at an upcoming conference in Auckland she spent either at the pool or the gym. When she did come home she was as tired as he was after his nights on call, so it seemed that, instead of having more time together, the time they did have now was spent in bed.

He knew it was ludicrous to feel resentment at the arrangement—given that it had been his idea in the first place—but knowing how absurd the feeling was didn't make it any less real.

'How about we go away this weekend?' he asked on Wednesday morning over breakfast. 'We could fly across to Blenheim Friday night and pick up a rental car.' Blenheim, a town near the top of South Island, was the hub of the area's wine district and a short drive from the scenic beauty of the Marlborough Sounds. 'Leslie's brother's got a bach right on the water with a boat we can use.' He'd stayed at the holiday house years ago with Leslie, and she'd reminded him of it the day before and had told him that he was welcome to use it. 'It'd be nice to spend a couple of days lazing about. If we get energetic we can tour a few vineyards. Hmm?'

'Sam, that does sound nice.' But he knew from the hurried way she dumped her cereal bowl into the sink then whirled around and kissed him that it hadn't been nice enough. 'But I absolutely must work this weekend. I'm going to Auckland on Tuesday, remember. This weekend's the last chance I have to get my talk organised.'

'Bring your work with you.' He caught her arm as she

went to turn away. 'You can sit by the water and work. It'll be fun.'

'It'd be lovely but I need my computer and the Net and so many books…' She bent over and kissed him again. 'Can we do it another time?'

'Sure.' Given how many hours his own new job was demanding, he reminded himself again that any resentment of Cathie's work commitments was unreasonable. 'How about in three weeks?'

'Three weeks?' She frowned a little. 'That's going to be too soon, Sam. Look, I'll check my diary when I get to work. There's so much coming up in the next month or two… I'll find a good time and let you know for sure.'

'OK.' He'd leave it to her. He squeezed her hand, then used it to draw her into his arms. 'Just don't forget. It'll be good for us both to get away from other distractions for a couple of days.'

'We haven't had much time,' she agreed softly. 'Work seems pretty hectic for both of us at the moment.'

'I thought living together would bring us closer,' he murmured. 'I thought we'd have more time. But we don't. The only change seems to be more sex.'

'Hey!' She drew back, her face mock-shocked. 'What are you saying? Is this Sam Wheatley, complaining about too much sex?'

'I didn't say *too* much,' he protested. 'And I'm not complaining. I'm just saying that I thought there'd be more…' He hesitated, searching for the explanation he wanted. 'I suppose ''intimacy'' is the right word. Intimacy's different to sex.'

'OK.' But he thought she looked puzzled. 'I'll work on it. Sorry, Sam. I promise we'll have more time soon. Much more time. By next month I'll have Auckland and the Arizona convention out of the way—'

'Arizona?' Sam pulled back. 'Hang on a minute, Cat.'

This was the first mention he'd heard of something happening outside New Zealand. '*Arizona* Arizona?'

'Tucson, Arizona,' she said slowly, her face stiffening. 'Sam—'

'You're going to the States?' And she hadn't told him? 'When?'

'A few days after I get back from Auckland,' she said unevenly. 'They haven't given us our tickets yet so I don't know the exact date. All top sales staff are going, and for the first time that means four of us from Wellington. It's going to be great, Sam. It's a chance to catch up with international trends—'

'Cathie, you never mentioned this.'

'We were only told a couple of weeks ago ourselves. That night you threw Martin out, that was the other part of what we'd all been celebrating, along with the sales figures. I meant to tell you…'

'How long will you be away?'

'The convention only lasts a week but some of us are thinking about staying on another fortnight or so to visit a few sites and shadow some of the company's American representatives. We're still waiting for the approvals to come through but the opportunity to see the American operation is such a valuable one that I've said I'll take one of the weeks as annual leave if necessary so there shouldn't be a problem.'

Three weeks! 'So, including the five days in Auckland, you'll be away a month?'

'More or less,' she said slowly. 'Is that a problem?'

'The problem is you didn't seem to think it important to tell me,' Sam said through gritted teeth. He couldn't object to the demands of her work but he sure as hell objected to her treating his place in her life so casually that she hadn't thought he needed to know she was leaving the country in two weeks. 'Why haven't you said something?'

Some change, some faint stiffening in her expression and the fraction of a second that her eyes flickered away from him made him certain that, despite her casualness, she hadn't simply forgotten but instead had kept her plans from him deliberately. 'Who else is going from Wellington?'

'David, Kyle McInnes and Martin.'

His teeth gritted again at the last name she mentioned. 'I thought Martin had only just started. How did he manage to get top sales?'

'He's a transfer from Auckland. The sales figures were calculated over twelve months.'

'Cathie—'

'I knew you'd overreact,' she said defensively, stepping away from him. 'Poor Martin told me how you beat him up that night—'

'I didn't touch him,' he interrupted, more than exasperated by the accusation, although if he had his chance again he thought Martin's behaviour might warrant it. 'I even put him to bed. Didn't he tell you that?'

'He said he was covered in bruises.'

'He might have got the odd bruise,' Sam conceded, prepared to admit that. He hadn't exactly handled the creep gently, but neither, despite the temptation, had he laid into him. 'But, much as he was asking for it, I didn't thump him.'

'Sam, you're so much stronger than him that it would have only taken one punch—'

'I don't,' Sam said tersely, 'throw punches. I will admit that I have never been so tempted to hit another human being, but I didn't cheapen myself on that idiot.' But the defensiveness of her expression hadn't changed and he shook his head. 'Believe what you like,' he said heavily.

'Of course I believe you,' she said finally after a silence that had him feeling sick. 'Martin does exaggerate things, I suppose. I think he's been feeling like some sort of hero with his stories around the office about being thrown about by my boyfriend.'

'Oh, he does admit now that you have a boyfriend, does he?' Sam asked dryly.

She smiled. 'I think he understands that now.'

'Good. If he forgets again I'm happy to remind him.'

'I'm sorry I didn't explain.'

'What I don't understand is how you didn't even mention this trip,' he said sadly. 'Cathie, this is a big thing to keep to yourself. Even if we hadn't been living together I'd have expected you to tell me that.'

'I thought you might want to veto it,' she said quietly.

'Veto it?' That startled him. 'What are you talking about?'

'You gave me an ultimatum to get me here,' she said gingerly. 'What's to stop you doing the same thing about my work?'

'No.' The idea that she'd feared that appalled him. 'Why would I ever...? Cathie, I'd never do that. I'd never expect you to choose between me and your career.' The suggestion was absurd. 'I know how much your work means to you.' Besides, even if he had any right to impose his opinion on her, he suspected that in any contest between her work and him he would come in a fairly distant second. 'And why on earth would I want to prevent you going on a business trip?'

'I thought you might not want me going away.'

'I might not like being alone very much but that doesn't mean I'm about to stop you,' he declared flatly. 'Cathie, I like it that you enjoy your work. I wouldn't ever suggest you do something which might hinder your career.'

'But what about Martin? He'll be there, Sam. He's one of the people hoping to stay on for the two weeks afterwards.'

He felt his teeth grit for the umpteenth time. 'I must

admit that the thought of him going off to America with you is not a pleasant one,' he grated. 'And I don't trust him one millimetre. But I trust you. That is as long as you promise me you won't let him jump into bed with you again.'

'I promise,' she said softly. She kissed him, a long, warm, loving kiss that made his pulse thud. 'I'm sorry I didn't tell you sooner. I love you.'

He took her chin and held her while he returned her kiss. 'So marry me and we'll live happily ever after and have dozens of children.'

'Dozens!' Her nose wrinkling, she drew back, laughing. 'Dream on.' Whether she meant about the marriage, or the dozens, or about any children at all, she didn't stop to say. 'I have to dash,' she said breathlessly, bending to scoop up her bag as she swept out of the room. 'I'm very, very late. I'll be home late tonight so don't wait up. Bye, Sam.'

The door slammed before he had a chance to answer.

On the unit, Daniel Williams had made a little progress. It was more than two weeks since his tracheostomy tube had been inserted. He was awake now—Sam had reduced his sedation immediately after the tracheostomy surgery—and, although he still required ventilation and had no voluntary movement in any of his limbs, he could blink to communicate. There was also evidence that his vital capacity—the amount of air his lungs could hold—was increasing. 'Which is a good sign,' he told the couple, standing back after completing his examination. 'It's very good news.'

'The physiotherapists are pleased with his arms,' Mrs Williams told him. 'They seem to feel things are starting to get better, too.'

Sam nodded. The physiotherapists had been working with Mr Williams intensely since his admission—with both his chest, helping it to clear secretions, and with his back and limbs, keeping his muscles supple and active to prevent contractures developing in them while he remained paralysed.

'His blood pressure and pulse have been very settled,' she added.

'They have,' Sam agreed. Most of the signs of autonomic nerve disturbances had stabilised, although that was no guarantee that they'd stay that way. 'Also we've been able to cut down on the amount of pain relief we're giving, which is another good sign.'

Guillain-Barré could be a painful syndrome, with sufferers describing the limb and back pain that commonly accompanied it as akin to the pain of a prolapsed spinal disc. In the first two weeks they'd been using high-dose opiates, as well as anti-inflammatory medication, to control any discomfort, but they'd been able to reduce the opiate dose considerably over the past week. 'All the signs are promising,' Sam concluded.

'We were beginning to think nothing would ever change,' Mrs Williams said weakly.

'It may still be weeks before Daniel is ready to breathe on his own again,' he warned. 'Then the weakness in his legs may take much longer to improve, sometimes more than a year, and, as the neurologist was saying yesterday, there's no guarantee that he'll recover full function.'

'But the signs today are good,' she said quickly.

'The signs today are good,' he agreed with a smile. 'Yes.' He was optimistic. 'Fingers crossed.'

Jill Harkness, their young patient who'd fractured her pelvis when her car had hit a power pole, was having a stormy few weeks. Despite their determined efforts to flush fluid through her kidneys after her admission to hospital, the organs had suffered from the combined effects of the huge amount of trauma she'd had—one of the breakdown products of her injured muscles had damaged her kidneys—

and the blood loss and low blood pressure she would have had after the crash and during the time it had taken rescue workers to get to her.

She needed dialysis—where her blood was filtered through a machine to remove toxins—every second day. He'd hoped that by now her kidneys would have recovered enough of their function to be able to reduce that frequency, but her morning's blood results weren't good.

'At this stage it's still impossible to say if the kidney problems will be long term,' he told her parents. 'There's still a chance that they'll recover.'

'What about her lungs, Doctor?' Her mother was watching her sadly. 'The nurse said that they were about the same this morning.'

'There hasn't been any change overnight,' he agreed, adding quickly, when he saw their obvious despair, 'but that is a good thing with ARDS.' ARDS, or adult respiratory distress syndrome, a condition where the lung tissue grew too leaky to work properly, was a dangerous complication of major injuries. 'It means she's stable,' he explained. 'We haven't needed to increase the amount of oxygen we're giving her. That's a very good sign. If we can stop things from getting worse and hold things level until her lungs get a chance to recover then we're on the right track.'

'I really thought we were going to lose her at the weekend,' her mother said softly. 'When we got that phone call…?'

Sam nodded. He'd asked her nurse to make that call at about two on Sunday morning when Jill's lung function had reached its lowest point despite maximum therapy. The mortality of ARDS was high and there'd been a few hours there when he'd feared he wasn't going to be able to pull things around. 'Things are looking much better today than they were on Sunday,' he told them gently. 'She's young and she's strong. That has to be on her side.'

Leslie was waiting at the main desk when he finished with Jill. 'Hi. Thought you might like to know about Mrs Robinson.'

'Come for coffee,' he said smoothly. Pointedly ignoring Tim's interested look, along with the mock leer the nurse made at Leslie's back, he held out his arm to direct the psychiatrist into the side corridor leading to the unit's staff-room. 'Mrs Robinson?'

'The lady with the carbon monoxide poisoning,' she reminded him while he made their drinks. 'She'd been depressed about her difficulty in getting pregnant.'

'Her husband found her in the car,' he said, remembering. He added boiling water to their mugs then turned around. 'Don't tell me she's taken another overdose this month?'

She sent him a disapproving look. 'Not a nice comment on my psychiatric skills,' she said mockingly. 'No, I wanted to reassure you that she's doing fine.'

He smiled. 'Good. Milk and sugar?'

'Neither.' She took the mug he offered her. 'Her gynae investigations haven't shown up anything and she's been prescribed a holiday,' she told him. 'Her husband's taking her up to the Bay of Islands for a week. I suspect they both need the break. But that's not the only reason I wanted to see you. I wanted to invite you and Cathie to my house-warming.' She gave him the date for the Saturday a month ahead. 'I thought I'd get my invitations out early so people would be free.'

Sam frowned. 'I'm not on call that weekend but Cathie will be away.'

'You're allowed to come alone.' She'd kicked off her shoes and now she lifted her stockinged feet and tucked them under her on the chair, the brevity of her tight skirt meaning that he couldn't help but notice that Leslie still had extraordinarily good legs. An attribute, he recalled dryly, of which she was particularly proud.

She recited a few names of other doctors and nurses he knew who'd be there. 'I promise not to actually lunge at you myself if that makes you more likely to turn up single, although, of course, I can't make any guarantees for any of the other women.'

Sam laughed. He suspected that the days of women lunging at him were long past. 'I wouldn't remember what to do,' he said easily. 'It's been a long time since anyone even flirted with me.'

'Huh. You just don't notice. I imagine women flirt with you all the time.' She finished her drink quickly then uncoiled her legs and slid her feet into her shoes. 'I didn't realise how late it was getting. I'd better run.' She took a card out of her pocket and passed it to him. 'That's the address and number. Call me if you need to know anything. How long is Cathie going to be away?'

'Around a month in total. She's flying to Auckland on Tuesday and after that she's going away again.' He explained about Cathie's high sales figures having earned her the trip to Arizona.

Leslie tilted her head. 'You sound like a proud father.'

'Well, I'm hardly paternal but I am proud, I suppose.' He stilled. The recognition of the feeling surprised him, but she was right. He was proud of Cathie's achievements. He guided Leslie out of the staffroom and back towards the main part of the unit. 'She's very good at her job.'

'Just as long as she's not neglecting you,' she said smoothly. She squeezed his arm, her fingers lingering a little. 'If you get a craving for feminine company, give me a call, Sam. Since I'm not seeing anyone at present we could spend a few warm nights catching up on some good memories.'

'I'll let you know.' Sam wondered if she was teasing him, but although her eyes sparkled her face was straight and he wasn't sure how seriously to take her. He waved his hand to activate the sensor which opened the main doors. 'Thanks, Leslie. And thanks for letting me know about Mrs Robinson.'

When he turned around from seeing her off, Tim was there, his beam and raised brows suggesting he'd caught Leslie's cryptic invitation. 'Well, that was a brazen pass if I've ever heard one,' he said cheerfully. 'She's a bit of a stunner, too. Smitten, Sam?'

'Not with Leslie,' Sam said slowly. He frowned at the door through which the psychiatrist had left. 'You really think that was a pass?'

'With bells and whistles,' Tim told him.

Leslie really was getting desperate. 'We're very old friends.'

'You've got to watch out for women these days, Sam.' The other man was grinning again. 'They're man-eaters.'

'Not all of them,' he said heavily.

'Trust me.' The charge nurse was still grinning. 'And, Sam, I'd get your head out of the sand. If you're really not keen on the sexy psychiatrist, don't take her up on her invitation. I wouldn't want to see you ending up in a whole lot of trouble with your other love.'

But Sam wondered. He doubted if Cathie would even notice.

CHAPTER SEVEN

THE days before Cathie's US trip flew past. Sam was supposed to be on call at Kapiti on her last night in town, but he managed to swap with one of the other anaesthetists on the ICU roster so that he could spend some time with her. However, she rang him at home soon after he arrived to say that she was still stuck in a briefing session and not to wait on her for tea, and in the end they only had a few hours together.

Next morning she waved aside his suggestion that he drive her to the airport. 'Sam, I don't expect you to do that.' He'd just stepped out of the shower and she was packing the last of her things into her suitcase, but she spun around and shook her head firmly. 'You've got to get to work. Besides, I've already ordered a taxi.'

'Then I'll cancel it.' He fastened a towel around his hips and headed for the phone at the side of the bed. 'I'll get onto it now. Which company?'

'But the airport's miles out of your way. You'll be late.'

'It'll only take twenty minutes,' he said evenly. Wellington's airport was situated in the city's south-eastern suburbs, relatively close to where they lived. 'And the unit knows I'll be late. I warned Phillipa yesterday. Which taxi company?'

'Sam.'

'Cathie.' He mimicked her impatient tone with a smile. 'I don't mind. I want to see you off.'

'But I mind,' she protested. 'I'm fine, honestly. I'm quite capable of getting myself to the airport. We've said goodbye in the important way.'

'We've made love,' he said dryly. But although he masked his expression, her comment unsettled him because it wasn't the first time she'd made sex sound like a vastly more significant part of their interaction than the emotional intimacy he craved. 'We haven't said goodbye,' he pointed out. 'I haven't waved you off, and I want to. Cat, it's only a short drive.'

'I want to take a taxi.'

'Why?'

'Why not?' He saw her eyes starting to spark.

'This is so trivial it's not worth arguing about,' he said soothingly. 'I'm very happy to drive you. Why are you being so stubborn?'

'It's you who's stubborn,' she came back sharply, startling him. 'Don't you dare call me stubborn. There's only one stubborn person out of the two of us and that's you. You're the most stubborn person I've ever met. You just push and push until you get what you want. Thank you for your offer, Sam.' She said the words as if they hurt her. 'But no. I'm taking a taxi and that's the end of it.'

Sam froze, stunned by the vehemence of her attack, but, even knowing that the sensible thing would be to give in and let her do what she wanted, he couldn't let it rest. 'Cathie, I don't want to say goodbye like this.'

'You don't have any choice.' She threw the last of her things into her suitcase with an abruptness that betrayed her annoyance. She pulled the lid down over the over-stuffed case then glared at him when he went to help her. 'I can do it,' she snarled. 'Leave it alone. I'm not so feeble I can't shut my own case.'

He recoiled. 'I didn't say—'

'You didn't have to,' she raged. 'It's blazingly obvious what you think. It's written all over your face.'

'That's unfair,' he grated, sharp himself now. 'I'm trying to help—'

'Don't,' she retorted. 'I don't need you to help me.' Clicking the snaps of her case shut, she hauled it off the bed, but the furious look she sent him as he again went forward involuntarily to help her was enough to stop him in his tracks. 'I can manage.'

Not very well, he wanted to say, wincing at the way the case banged against her leg as she dragged it, as well as her overnight bag, and handbag and coat, towards the door.

He discarded his towel, pulled on the jeans he'd left thrown across the dresser the night before and followed her as she thumped the suitcase down his stairs. 'Cathie, this is ludicrous,' he said quietly, when she still didn't look at him but instead just opened the front door and dragged her things outside. 'What's wrong?'

'Everything's wrong,' she cried. 'Everything.' She put her case and bags down then wiped the palms of both her hands over her eyes. When she took them away Sam saw the smudged make-up and the glittering moisture that had turned her eyes brilliant green. 'I'm sorry, Sam. Everything's been wrong for weeks. Surely you can see that. I've been waiting for this. I knew something like this would happen.'

'Something like what?' he asked huskily, distressed by her tears. It wasn't the first time he'd seen her cry—she was often moved by sad events in the news or cases they both encountered through their work or problems with her mother—but he'd never seen her weeping for herself or for him. 'Do you mean something like us arguing?'

He wanted to go to her, wanted to offer some sort of…comfort, whatever he could do that might help, but she'd stretched one hand out towards him as if to fend him off.

'It doesn't matter,' he soothed. 'It's not important. Couples argue all the time. It's normal. And I understand that you might feel as if by living here you're losing some of your independence, as if I'm taking that away, but we need to talk through that. What matters is how we deal with our problems, how we work through them together.'

'But I don't want to deal with it.' Not looking at him, she pulled tissues out of her bag and wiped her eyes and blew her nose. 'I don't need this. I don't need this stress in my life.'

'What stress?' He was still bewildered. 'The stress of living with me?'

'Sam, it isn't working.' She swept an arm around as if to encompass both his house and him. 'I knew it wouldn't but...I let you persuade me. I feel as if I'm on tenterhooks all the time. I keep waiting for things to go wrong. I can't go on like that. It distracts me, stops me from all the important things I should be thinking about. I made a mistake. I think we should...I think we should use these three weeks to do some hard thinking about what it is we both want.'

He didn't need three weeks. He didn't even need three minutes. 'Cathie, I know what I want,' he said heavily. 'Don't leave like this.'

'I have to, Sam.' It was still half an hour before he'd thought they'd need to leave for the airport, but she was checking the street behind him, as if expecting the taxi to arrive at any moment. 'I'm sorry. I think it's best.'

'Best for who—?' But the low sound of an approaching engine brought him swinging around, and he saw a taxi turn the corner.

Only as it drew closer and Cathie began collecting her things together did he realise that the driver of the taxi wasn't the only person in the car. Bending as it came to a stop, Sam glared at the man who'd now squashed himself up in the rear seat as if to get as far away as possible from him and who clearly had no intention of leaping out to greet either of them. 'Cathie—'

She didn't let him finish. 'Goodbye, Sam.' Her eyes

flickered over him so briefly that they could have been casual acquaintances, saying farewell to each other. The driver had come around to help her and Sam observed bitterly that she clearly didn't feel that letting *him* take her case threatened her independence in any way. 'I'll let you know when I get back about collecting my things.'

Sam felt as if he'd been kicked in the stomach. Slowly, very slowly, he took a step back, keeping his expression fiercely guarded. 'You're moving out?'

'I'm sorry.' He'd never seen her so pale but her tears had dried and her small chin had a firmly determined set. 'I wish it could have been different.'

Each word was like another thud against his heart. He sent the man who still sat huddled and quiet against the back seat of the taxi a harsh look. 'Is it him?'

'Martin?' To his relief she looked genuinely startled by the idea. 'No. Of course it's not. There's no one else. It's nothing like that.'

Then she was opening the door to climb in beside the other man and there was no time left. The driver had finished stowing her things. He went around to the front and started the engine, and the car drew away, without Cathie looking at Sam again.

Somehow he managed to get through the next week. Work, at least, was there to distract him, but coming home was hard. Although Cathie had been there less than a month, every room, every space seemed imbued with the essence and memory of Cathie. He'd owned the house more than a decade and it seemed profoundly unfair that a mere four weeks of Cathie had altered it so perceptibly.

Midway through the following week he called Will but Maggie answered instead. 'He's playing golf,' she explained. 'Since he's due back at work next week he's getting a decent game in while he can. Am I any use to you, Sam, or do you have to speak to him?'

He explained that he'd had a few more thoughts about selling his house and her tone was delighted as she told him to come for tea. 'Any time,' she insisted when he prevaricated. 'It doesn't matter—just whenever you finish on the unit. Will shouldn't be late.'

However, when he got there Maggie explained that she was still alone. When she'd opened the door to him, her expression had turned briefly searching, but when he reached forward, one arm outstretched, she smiled and passed him Timothy to hold while she took the flowers he'd brought out of his other arm.

'Thank you,' she said with a smile. 'They're beautiful. Will won't be long. He called ten minutes ago as he was leaving. He was held up *unexpectedly* at the nineteenth hole.' She turned and rolled her eyes a little at him as she laughed. 'Sam, you look good with a baby.'

'It feels good,' Sam conceded, bouncing Timothy against his chest slightly as he followed her. 'I love babies. I love watching how quickly they change. He's growing so fast.'

'I can't see it.' She was filling a brightly coloured vase with water. 'I can feel that he's heavier, but to me he still looks the same.'

'Oh, he's smiling!' Sam exclaimed warmly, thrilled by the baby's delight as he stared up at him. 'Timothy, what a big smile.'

'He's been smiling for two weeks now,' Maggie confirmed with a pleased laugh. 'Isn't he gorgeous? I can see Will in him so strongly when he does that.' Leaving the flowers, she came across to stand with them, and they cooed together for a few minutes, then she went quiet. 'Sam, are you all right?'

He looked up at her sharply. 'Of course.'

She hesitated for a few seconds. 'You don't look it.'

'We had a busy night on call last night.'

'You haven't been on continually the past month.'

He winced. 'That bad?'

'Either that or a very hard case of the flu,' she said evenly. 'And you're not sneezing. I don't mean to pry, Sam. It would just be good to hear that you're OK.'

'Maggie, I'm barely sure of that myself.' He wasn't used to talking about the way he felt with anyone but Cathie, but the urge to unburden at least some of his turmoil was almost overwhelming. He looked down into Timothy's little face. 'Cathie's leaving me. She's away in North America at a convention but she's due back in a week and...well, I managed to persuade her to move into the house a few weeks ago but now she's moving out again.'

'Oh, Sam.' She put her arm around his back. 'I'm so sorry. I was wondering after she said she didn't want to be Timothy's godmother, but you seemed so happy together that night. Do you think it's just a temporary setback?'

'I don't know.' He barely knew anything any more. He hadn't heard a thing from her since the day she'd left for the airport, and the way her boss had refused to give him any information about where his employees were staying suggested Cathie had left instructions for Sam not to be told anything.

He passed Timothy to Maggie and when she sat he sank back onto the couch beside her. 'Things haven't been right for a long time,' he admitted heavily. He passed his hand across his face. 'Maggie, I thought everything was supposed to be all right when you loved each other. I thought that saying "I love you" meant everything was going to be happy ever after. Cathie's the first woman I've ever loved, but instead of marriage and children and bliss for the rest of our lives it's as if falling in love with each other hasn't changed a thing. She says that she loves me but it still doesn't work.'

He closed his eyes. 'I had a call yesterday from her ex-flatmate, complaining that Cathie had left the country without remembering to pay her share of next month's rent. Susan needs the money to pay the landlord and she wanted to know if I could lend it to her until Cathie gets back.

'Maggie, she's still been keeping her lease up on the flat. Susan told her that she was happy to find someone to take over her room, but Cathie wouldn't let her. Obviously, she never committed herself to staying with me. All this time I've been thinking that if I just took things slowly, didn't push her, she'd realise how wonderful it could be, being together, and she'd understand that there was nothing to be frightened about in commitment. But all that time she wasn't happy at all. She didn't expect things to work out. She was always planning to leave.'

'It sounds as if Cathie has some problems of her own to work through,' Maggie said gently. 'She's said the odd thing about her parents fighting when she was young and about them being married so many times since. It wouldn't be surprising if her upbringing meant she was wary of committing herself.'

'I've tried to raise that but she won't listen to me,' he said quietly, looking at her. 'She calls it my psychiatrist's hat. She jokes about how all doctors think that a few weeks on a psychiatry ward as medical students makes us think we're all Sigmund Freuds. She hates it when she thinks I'm trying to analyse her.'

'Still, it makes sense.'

'I don't know.' He'd thought about it a lot. 'Isn't it more likely that an unsettled upbringing like hers would make someone crave stability?'

'Unless, by committing herself to someone, she feels she's leaving herself open to hurt because she assumes he'll always tire of her and move on to another partner,' Maggie said gently.

Sam conceded the possibility of that. 'But after two years she must know me well enough to understand that would never happen,' he mused. 'She knows my family. There hasn't been a divorce in the Wheatley family in seventy years.'

'What about relationship counselling?'

He almost choked. 'About as much chance of getting Cathie into that as getting Timothy here to drive me home tonight,' he said ruefully. He stroked the baby's forehead. 'She's allergic to therapists. I think that she was forced into family therapy when she was young when her parents' marriage first started falling apart and it put her off for life.'

'But she loves you. And you've been together for two years. That must mean she has some strong feelings about your relationship. Perhaps if she thought the counselling would help you stay together…?'

'The two years isn't so significant,' he revealed. 'I've been thinking about that a lot lately. I've been wondering if she hasn't just been staying for the…physical side of our relationship.' The admission wasn't easy and he leaned forward, his arms resting on his knees as he studied the floor in front of them. 'Maggie, I don't know. Sex seems to be Cathie's answer to everything these days. That's supposed to be a woman's complaint, rather that a man's, isn't it?'

He slanted her a smile that was only half-amused. 'But Leslie said something to me a few weeks ago about…' He remembered the psychiatrist's amused reference to him being treated like a sex object, 'Well, she just said something that made me look at things more carefully. I told Cathie once that it bothered me that we seemed to be substituting sex for intimacy, but she just gave me a funny look and I knew she had no idea what I meant.'

'I hope you both manage to work things out,' Maggie said softly. 'You obviously love her very much.'

'Oh, Maggie.' He couldn't even describe how much.

'When she walks into the room I dissolve,' he said roughly. 'When she smiles it's as if I'm in heaven.'

'Sam, you don't show it,' she said huskily. 'When you're with Cathie you always seem to me to be very cool and amused. If you hadn't talked to me now I'd never have guessed how strongly you felt about her. Are you sure she understands?'

'I've told her often enough,' he said heavily. He'd never played games with Cathie and he'd never concealed his feelings from her.

'Sam, I mean this in the best possible way.' She touched his arm gently. 'Both Will and I think Cathie is lovely, but you do realise that if things don't work out with her there are plenty of other women—'

Sam groaned. 'Don't,' he said feelingly. 'Maggie, don't.' He still couldn't conceive of his life without Cathie yet, but even so he'd come to a small understanding over the past weeks that he wouldn't have to spend the rest of his life in solitude if he didn't choose to. He even managed a grin. 'Some of those nurses on the unit don't leave much room for doubt about their intentions.'

Maggie laughed. 'They're fun, aren't they? You know, I think they still give Will a bit of a hard time. I catch even him blushing sometimes. They're a wild bunch.'

'They are fun,' he agreed.

'And that night you were here we thought Leslie seemed rather intrigued,' Maggie added. 'Will mentioned that she used to be very keen on you years ago. I wouldn't be surprised if she still was.'

'*Very* keen is an exaggeration,' Sam responded, but he acknowledged that she could be right about Leslie still harbouring some interest in him. The psychiatrist had been persistent in her demands that he attend her house-warming at the weekend, and although he'd not mentioned anything more to her about Cathie, beyond the fact that she was away, Leslie's frequent phone calls and inappropriate visits to the unit were making it fairly plain that she was available should he choose to take an interest in the fact.

Tim, a shrewd observer of such antics, had been hugely entertained by her visits that week, and in the last few days Sam had begun to agree that the nurse was probably right in his assessment of the situation.

'It is a little like balm for my battered ego,' Sam confessed, faintly shamed by that fact, 'but the nurses on the unit aren't serious, and much as I like Leslie there's no romance there.'

He spent the Monday that Cathie was due back in Wellington in tense expectation of a call from her, but he heard nothing before leaving the unit that evening and his mobile was silent all the way back into town. She still had the key he'd given her so it wasn't an impossible scenario that she'd arrived back and had already collected the rest of her things from his house. However, when he pulled up outside her car was there and she was sitting on the top step, waiting for him.

His heart pounding, he climbed out of the car and went slowly towards her, noting uneasily the absence of any luggage apart from her day pack. 'Hi.'

'Hi.' She stood up slowly, her expression so guarded and formal it made him ache.

'You look great.' Although the compliment was sincere, he was aware that it might sound clichéd but he wasn't sure how else to approach her. Her expression certainly didn't suggest that she'd welcome him embracing her. Cathie normally took scrupulous care to protect herself from the sun but in the three weeks she'd been away she'd acquired a light tan. 'The colour suits you.'

'The ozone layer over there is thicker,' she said stiffly.

'I thought getting a little bit of colour wouldn't be as dangerous. How have you been?'

He didn't answer that. 'How was your trip? Why are you waiting out here? You could have gone inside.'

'The trip was fine. It was a long flight back and we were delayed in Auckland, but I managed to get a few hours' sleep. I rang you at work and the nurse told me you'd left so I knew I wouldn't have long to wait. It didn't feel right going inside when you weren't here.'

He sent her a vaguely impatient look. Taking care not to brush by her, he went up to the door and opened it. 'I missed you.'

'I'm sorry.' He hadn't wanted an apology, but he'd got one anyway. 'Sam, I think it's best if we leave the talking for another time when we're both feeling less emotional. I'm here to collect my things.'

He sighed. 'Cathie—'

'Please, don't make this more difficult than it already is for me.' She tilted her little face up to him so calmly and determinedly—and in a way so typical of her—that he had to fight the insane urge to take her in his arms and kiss her senseless. 'I don't want it to be like this either, but we've already said everything that needed to be said about me living here.'

Then why did he feel as if they'd hardly ever talked? He waited until they were inside with the door closed behind them. 'Cathie, I love you. Stay. You don't have to leave.' He still had Maggie's suggestion at the front of his mind and although he thought he knew how she'd react he didn't have anything else to try. 'We could see someone—'

'A counsellor?' She sent him a strained look. 'Sam, the last thing I need right now is some do-gooder with a diploma in playing with people's minds to tell me what's wrong with our relationship.'

'So tell me,' he demanded, impatience overriding his determination to take things carefully. 'Since you know it all, tell me. Because, Cathie, you've mystified me. I haven't got a clue.'

'Don't start.'

'Yes, I'm going to start.' Her appeal was absurd. There was too much at stake for him to let her go without a fight. 'Talk to me, Cat. Tell me what's going on.'

'What's going on is that we can't live together,' she said stiffly. 'I love you, too, Sam. But moving in together was a mistake.'

'Am I so bad?'

'Of course you're not.' Mystifyingly, his comment seemed to puzzle her because she looked confused. 'It's not you. You're wonderful. You're always wonderful. It's nothing to do with you. It's just that I always knew that me living here wasn't going to work—'

'You haven't given it a chance.' He knew they'd had problems, he'd given enough thought himself to the lack of intimacy in their relationship, but they hadn't had time to work through that. 'You were only here a few weeks,' he reminded her. He knew he wasn't reaching her and that was frustrating him. 'And we were both so busy we hardly saw each other in that time.'

'I shouldn't have come in the first place,' she argued. 'I always knew it would be a disaster. If it hadn't been for you getting furious about Martin that night—'

'Are you still angry about me kicking that weasel out of your bed?' he demanded savagely.

'Martin says that the way you treated him proves that you're—'

'Don't you dare quote that bast—'

'Hurling abuse won't change anything,' she raged back. 'And Martin has two parents, thank you very much. I've met them.'

He stopped himself from demanding where and when and why. 'So this is about Martin?'

'No,' she shouted. 'You're obsessed with him.'

'I'm not obsessed,' he raged. 'It's you who keeps bringing him up.'

'The poor man's never done a thing to you.'

Right then he'd have cheerfully wrung the 'poor' man's neck. 'Cathie, this is insane. Arguing about that...idiot is insane.' He ran his hand around the back of his neck and arched his back to try and release some of the tension. 'Where are you getting this?' he demanded, deliberately lowering his tone to something he hoped sounded more reasonable, although there was nothing reasonable about the way he was feeling. 'I've never tried—'

He broke off, the blazing green of the eyes that had followed the movement of his hand and her compulsive swallow stilling him. 'Is this exciting you?' he demanded.

Her eyes flew to his face and he noted the widened darkness of her pupils with a mixture of appalled recognition and desire.

'It's been three weeks,' she said thickly. 'Regardless of my personal feelings, naturally I'm a little sensitive to you—'

'Don't.' Sam reeled away lest she realise his own abrupt response to her. 'I don't believe it. Cathie, don't.'

'It's normal.'

'It's *not* normal.' He didn't know who he was more disgusted at. Her, for being aroused by his anger? Or himself, for reacting to it as violently as he was doing? 'It's sick. We're trying to resolve something fundamental to our relationship here and you're thinking about sex?'

'We wouldn't be having any trouble now if you hadn't tried to make things more than sex in the first place,' she rasped.

'Maybe if you'd taken a little time to sort out whether

you actually wanted a man in your life or whether you couldn't have bought what you really crave from a sexual supply shop instead—' He broke off, knowing from her horrified gasp and her abrupt shocked pallor that he'd gone too far.

'I didn't mean to say that but it's how I feel,' he said huskily. He knew she didn't want it but he took her into his arms anyway, soothing his hands across her stiff back. 'The sick thing is, I almost want to keep you on those terms. I want you so much I could almost keep seeing you just for the sex.'

'Almost,' she echoed, her voice muffled against his chest.

'I'm not going to do it, Cathie.' He kept stroking her shoulders and her back, taking care to keep their hips apart in the faint hope of preserving his sanity. 'I can't give you what you want. Not just sex and no commitment. I want more.'

'Sam, it's the "more" that's destroying us. We were so happy. Why can't we go back to that?'

'It's too late.' Sam closed his eyes weakly, inhaling the delicious scent from her hair shamelessly, his head spinning from her closeness despite his determination not to give in. 'I've changed. Cathie, I think there's a way we can work this out.'

'Oh, Sam, I do want to try,' she said huskily. The admission seemed to weaken her and he felt her soften against him. 'I don't want to lose you. I just want to go back to the way we were.'

His hands were holding her arms, offering her comfort if she chose to accept it, but instead she moved her lower body against him, twisting to the left a little so that the tightened nub of one breast brushed his fingers.

Involuntarily his hand opened to surround it and he heard her make a soft sound. When he looked down he saw her eyes had closed and her face had smoothed into a languid mask.

He felt sick. 'Cat, don't.' He withdrew his hand sharply. It felt as if rocks were falling and covering the light he'd glimpsed briefly at the end of the tunnel. 'Not sex,' he rasped. 'Not now.'

'Sam…?' She opened her eyes slowly, as if she was having trouble understanding him. 'What? Don't stop.'

'I hadn't started,' he pointed out coldly, putting her away from him. Obviously she hadn't understood any of what he'd said. It occurred to him that she'd merely been leading him on in the hope that he'd give her what she wanted, and the thought made him sick. 'We can't talk now.' Not when she kept looking at him with those huge green eyes because soon, despite his disgust, he wouldn't be able to stop himself taking her in exactly the way she wanted.

'When we start talking is when we go wrong.' Her gaze dropped pointedly to below his waist. 'If you're trying to tell me you're not interested, Sam, you're wasting your time.'

'We're not animals, Cathie.' At least not on the surface. If she dug a little deeper that might change. 'You'd better go.'

She straightened. 'Half an hour ago you said you wanted me to stay with you. And you once accused *me* of being fickle?'

'I haven't changed my mind about loving you or wanting you here, but I've changed my mind about being available to you for sex,' he said heavily. 'If you really are sincere about wanting to sort out the problems in our relationship, then my solution is no sex.'

She looked appalled. 'Sam, I can't be with you and not think of sex.'

'Cathie, you can think about it all you want.' He smiled, almost laughed in his relief because her husky, desperate-sounding protest meant that there was hope that she might be at least prepared to seriously consider their future. For the first time in too long he caught a little glimpse of how it could be if he had some control of their relationship, and the sensation made him feel delirious. 'Think away. You're just not going to get any.'

CHAPTER EIGHT

'SAM, is that you whistling?' Tim shot him an astonished look when he arrived for his round the next morning. 'Don't tell me the old Sam's back again just when we were getting used to the gloomy one.'

'What?' Sam looked up from where he'd stopped to wash his hands, blinking. 'What are you talking about?'

The charge nurse and his registrar exchanged amused looks.

'You have been a bit brooding,' Phillipa said slowly.

'A *bit*?' Tim raised expressive brows. 'That's putting it mildly. Love of your life back from holidays, is she?'

Sam sent him a hard look. 'I didn't think I'd mentioned that she was away,' he said slowly, wondering where the charge nurse had got his information. 'But yes.' So to speak. Cathie wasn't back in his house but she was, at least, back in Wellington. 'Yes, she is.'

'Well, I know one sexy psychiatrist who's not going to be very happy about that,' Tim said. 'Not to mention a few dozen very disappointed nurses.'

Phillipa laughed but Sam rolled his eyes, guessing that Tim must have drawn his own conclusions about Cathie's absence based on Leslie's public attempts to persuade him along to her house-warming. He'd gone to the party out of politeness, but he hadn't stayed late. 'Any chance of getting some work done today or are we having a harass-the-consultant day?'

'Every day's a harass-the-consultant day,' chipped in Prue, the nurse looking after Daniel Williams for the morning. She batted her eyelashes mockingly at him on her way

124

past them towards the main nursing station. 'That's how we have fun around here.'

'That's not the only way,' Tim countered. 'There's a fair amount of harassing-the-charge-nurse that goes on around here, too. Don't let that one corner you in the equipment room,' he added, by way of a light aside to Sam. 'She's dangerous.'

Sam laughed. Given that Prue was happily married to one of his Wellington-based anaesthetic colleagues, he doubted whether he was in any serious danger.

'Where's Will?' he asked as they moved to start the round. The other consultant had returned to work the day before. 'Another day off?'

'In town for some administrative meeting,' Tim said cheerfully. 'He's due back after lunch.'

Sam nodded, remembering then that Will had mentioned something about the meeting on their last round.

Mr Williams was up in his chair, waiting for them with an expectant air. 'Still some residual proximal weakness,' the chief physiotherapist told them with a smile, 'but the neurologist yesterday was very pleased with his progress. If things continue to improve at this rate I expect Daniel to be walking within two to three weeks.'

'That's very good news,' Sam said, pleased. It was just over eight weeks since the day he'd had to admit him to the unit from Casualty. 'I think it's probably time that tube came out.' It had been a long, slow process, weaning their patient from the ventilator, but for the past two days he'd been breathing independently of the tube in his throat. 'What do you think, Tim?'

'We've just been waiting for the word,' the nurse said. 'All right, Daniel? We'll take it out today.'

Once the tube had been out for twenty-four hours they'd be able to make plans for him to leave the unit. 'Does the ward know?' Sam asked. 'All going well, you'll be able to

go to a medical ward tomorrow,' he added for Mr
Williams's benefit. 'Then you'll find out what rehab is really like.'

'We went down yesterday to have a look at the neurology and skin ward,' the physio said. 'Mr Williams seemed
quite impressed with everything.'

'Very nice,' their patient mouthed.

'We'll miss you,' Tim added with a smile. 'You've been
the stable force around the place lately.'

Sam nodded his agreement. The unit had been especially
busy over the past month. There had been a high turnover
of patients and their only two long-staying cases had been
transferred into new beds in the community. 'We haven't
had anyone in here more than two or three weeks, have
we?' he asked as they moved on to their next bed. 'Except
perhaps Jill Harkness.'

'Jill's been here seven weeks,' Phillipa confirmed.

But there was good news as far as Jill's results were
concerned. Her ARDS had resolved quickly once the initial
improvement had begun, and she'd now been off the ventilator for twenty-four hours and was breathing without difficulty. Along with the improvement in her respiratory
state, her renal function had gradually improved as well
over the previous fortnight.

'This morning's results look good,' Sam told her, surveying them. 'That potassium's stabilised beautifully.'
He'd already discussed the good news about Jill no longer
needing dialysis with both her and her parents, but the or-
thopaedic team were still looking after her broken leg and
pelvis. 'Are the orthopods happy for the transfer?'

'Going this morning,' Tim told him. 'How about it, Jill?
Ready to leave us?'

'Longing to leave you,' she said huskily. 'Not that I
don't love everybody,' she added with a smile. 'It's just
that I can have my friends to visit me on the normal ward.'

Sam smiled. 'That suits us, too,' he revealed. Part of the unit's infection control measures meant restricting visiting to immediate family only.

In Jill's case he and Tim had made an exception to allow her boyfriend to visit, but in the two or three days since she'd been well enough to appreciate visitors her other friends hadn't been allowed in. Forced to content themselves with waving from outside through the glass in the main doors, they'd made nuisances of themselves and he, along with the rest of the ICU staff, had been growing increasingly exasperated about having to make paths through the crowds to get into the unit. 'I had to fight my way through them to get home last night. You must be the most popular girl in town.'

She giggled. 'Not really. They're just being nice. They thought I was going to die.'

Sam exchanged an understanding look with Phillipa, remembering the nights they, too, had thought the same thing. Seeing someone survive the sort of trauma which would have been fatal in any other circumstances was one of the joys of ICU medicine for him.

Both in paediatric and adult ICU, there were times when it could be argued—when he thought himself even—that the expensive technology they employed seemed designed merely to delay inevitable death. But at other times, as with Jill, there were occasions when without that technology patients would certainly have died and thus the expense saved lives.

They'd had one admission the day before—a man who'd taken an overdose of his antidepressant medication. He'd needed ventilation and monitoring overnight, but was now breathing on his own and out of the danger period for any more of the heart arrhythmias that had caused problems the day before.

'He can go to the medics,' Sam declared, after examining

him. He looked through the chart where his nurse had pasted up the periods of abnormal heart rhythm he'd had overnight. 'Have the psychiatrists been up?'

'Yes, but, strangely enough, not Leslie Skinner,' Tim mused. 'We merely got the registrar on call, which I thought was rather puzzling because I was under the impression that Dr Skinner was going to look after our patients exclusively from now on.'

Sam eyed him neutrally. 'I expect the reason we've been seeing a lot of Dr Skinner is that she's a new appointment,' he ventured. 'She doesn't already have a heavy load of patients.'

Tim just grinned at him and continued the round. At the end they went back to the main nursing station where Sam wanted to check some X-rays, but the unit's ward clerk interrupted them by handing him a huge, Cellophane-enclosed bunch of flowers.

'For you, Sam. They went to Theatres before they came here.'

'Me?' Sam blinked. Mystified, but taking no notice of Tim's murmur about secret admirers, he unfastened the card. '"Thank you, Doctor, for all your help,"' he read. '"I'm told you saved my life. Bless you. From a lady with a heart that works now. Myra Daly."'

The name rang a bell but he couldn't place it and he frowned, trying to remember. 'Tim, have we had a patient called Myra Daly?' He showed him the card.

Shaking his head, the nurse reached for the unit's alphabetically listed discharge notebook. 'Doesn't ring any bells.'

'"With a heart that works,"' Phillipa echoed. 'Dr Wheatley, didn't you see a lady in day surgery a few weeks ago with aortic stenosis? I think I heard that she had a valve replacement a few days later in town.'

'Ah.' Sam remembered then and he was touched that

Mrs Daly had thought of him. 'I barely did anything,' he explained. 'I just referred her to one of the cardiologists. How thoughtful.'

He called Liz Stanton to check up on what had happened, and she confirmed the case Phillipa had outlined. 'She collapsed on the ward that night,' the cardiologist explained. 'She was resuscitated and scheduled for emergency surgery, did very well post-op and we discharged her yesterday. She's very lucky that she came in for her hernia that day.'

'Still whistling, Sam?' Tim sent him an amused look when Sam came back onto the unit after making the call.

'It just seems like a very good day,' Sam said easily. 'What's happening?'

'Phillipa and the SHO have skipped off to Casualty to see a woman with an asthma attack, but if you're in such a good mood how about Mr Swenson's arterial line? They were about to do it when they were called away.'

'Can't think of anything I'd rather be doing,' Sam told him. Simple procedures such as arterial lines tended to be the domain of the juniors on the unit, but he helped out readily if he was needed. Something he'd forgotten about adult ICU after his time in Neonates was just how hands-off adult work tended to be as a consultant. In Neonates he'd regularly carried out technical tasks, such as installing venous and arterial lines, but here the younger doctors managed most things independently. 'Does Phillipa's patient sound like one for us?'

'From what she said, it sounds as if the medical registrar just wants Phillipa's opinion to be on the safe side because the woman is very pregnant,' Tim said, shaking his head. 'She's not known to have severe asthma and she's never been in an ICU before.'

As Tim had predicted, Phillipa's patient didn't come to them. 'She's going to Obstetrics,' the registrar told him when she returned to the unit just as he was finishing Mr Swenson's radial artery line. 'Under joint care with the physicians who'll be looking after her chest.' She held the non-sterile end of the heparin pump line ready for Sam to connect it up.

'She's not too bad at the moment. I didn't think there was any need for you to see her. Her blood gases are good.' She told him the precise results. 'Obviously there was no need for her to come here,' she continued, and on the basis of the figures he agreed with that. 'At least not yet,' she added. 'I said we were happy to review if things changed.'

'How pregnant?'

'Thirty-five weeks.'

Sam nodded. Occasionally with severe asthma in late pregnancy it was necessary to deliver the baby by Caesarean section if the mother wasn't recovering, and although he had no reason to think that might have to happen in this case it was good to know that the baby would be mature enough to survive.

'I haven't seen many severe asthma attacks in pregnancy,' Phillipa added. 'I assumed that was because the hormones relaxed the airways enough to make them wider.'

'In about a third of cases asthma gets worse with pregnancy,' he told her as he shed his gown and wheeled the trolley he'd been using away from the bed. 'The other two thirds are fairly evenly divided between no change and an improvement.'

'In her last pregnancy she had no symptoms at all,' Phillipa said. 'Does that mean she's got a better chance of this attack staying mild?'

'No guarantee,' Sam said evenly.

He finished early that evening, managing to get away from Kapiti just after six. One effect of Cathie having been away almost a month was that he'd worked late often enough to catch up and keep up with most of his paperwork and reading.

As he drove back down the coast towards Wellington he caught himself whistling again a couple of times. The unconscious sign of a contented mind puzzled him because as far as he could make out he didn't have that much reason to be optimistic about Cathie. There'd been signs the night before that she was prepared to reconsider their relationship, true. But his refusal to acknowledge his sexual response to her had obviously frustrated her and she had left and hadn't contacted him since.

Once off the motorway he stopped for petrol. When he came back to the car, after paying, his mobile was ringing, but it stopped before he could open his bag. He had the same experience when he got to the house, hearing his telephone ringing and then his own voice speaking his recorded message, but he wasn't able to get the door unlocked and get inside in time for him to get to it before the machine shut off. The blinking number on it suggested he'd been rung at least six times, but when he played the tape back it was obvious that, whoever his caller had been, he or she had simply hung up after the tone without leaving any messages.

It wasn't unusual for him to have one or two non-messages like that a day—he'd always assumed that the problem was wrong numbers and that the callers hung up as soon as they realised the voice on his message wasn't the one they wanted—but six calls was exceptional.

Thoughtfully, he considered the thought that it might have been Cathie, but the idea was too novel to ring true. Cathie only occasionally called him—he invariably initiated most contacts—and if she did want to get hold of him she would have left a message.

He called the unit in case they needed him, but the nurse who answered assured him that all was well. 'We think we're taking someone from Coronary Care for monitoring overnight because they're full with a new admission due, but that hasn't been confirmed yet,' she said cheerfully. 'Sorry, Sam. Not us.'

'Thanks, Tina.' Assuming that his mystery caller would try again later, Sam left the phone and went upstairs to change into his running gear. Pushing himself, he ran up the hill and then along and down to the beach around Island Bay, before returning back into Newtown. He ran himself deliberately hard, enjoying the punishing rhythm, until the last couple of kilometres when he eased up, allowing his breathing to come back to near normal by the time he stopped outside the house.

Frowning, he saw when he got inside that there were two more non-messages on his machine. He filled a bottle of water from the tap in his kitchen, downed it, then called his parents. If something had happened to his father, his mother would, no doubt, want to tell him personally rather than leave a message.

But she assured him that his father was well. 'No change since the weekend, darling,' she said, when he apologised for calling them at their traditional teatime. 'Sam, you mustn't worry about him. He'd be upset if he thought you were worried. He's practically back to normal health, as far as I can see, and you yourself said he was sounding good on Saturday.

'It's been a glorious day and we've spent most of it in the garden around the house instead of out on the farm. We've finished planting out the new beds. We're having tea outside on the terrace tonight. It's still very warm. How's Cathie? Did she get back all right? Sam, it's ages since we've seen her. Why don't the two of you come up for a long weekend?'

'Work's busy for both of us at the moment, Mum.' His parents had a small farm about two hours' easy drive southwest of Auckland. He didn't explain about Cathie. There was hardly any point when he barely understood himself what was going on. 'I'm planning on driving up at Easter but I'll let you know if I get away for a few days before that.'

After talking briefly with his father, he went upstairs and adjusted the telephone beside his bed to maximum volume so that he'd hear it over the sound of the water when he was in the shower.

The phone rang just as he turned off the water. Grabbing for a towel, he ran into the bedroom and snatched it up on its second ring. 'Yes?'

'Oh.' At Cathie's soft sound he sank onto the bed, not caring that he was still streaming with water. 'You're there,' she added, sounding startled. 'I wasn't expecting you to pick up.'

Assuming from that comment that she'd been the one who'd been calling him earlier, he refrained from asking her why, then, she'd called yet again. He merely waited and after a few seconds she added, 'Can we meet, Sam?'

He hesitated. 'Here?'

'I thought in town.' Her answer came back so swiftly that he knew she must have already decided on that. She named a bar close to where she worked. It was a place she often went with her colleagues, and although it was more than a year since Sam had been there himself he remembered where it was. 'Fifteen minutes?'

'Make it twenty,' he said, considering his state of undress.

He was there in just under that but she was waiting for him at one of the high stools by the window. Unsure how their status had changed, he didn't kiss her as he would have normally but simply greeted her neutrally and asked if she wanted another drink.

'This is fine,' she said quietly, and he saw that the cappuccino in front of her had been barely touched.

He bought himself a beer and carried it back to where she was sitting.

'I gave a presentation at Keneparu today over lunch,' she said after he'd sat beside her, referring to one of the district's smaller hospitals. She mentioned the name of the antidepressant her company was trying to promote to the doctors who controlled the hospital's pharmaceutical lists. 'There's quite a lot of favourable information coming out of the American research at the moment about it. It was discussed a lot at the convention. We think it's going to be a front runner in future treatment. In fact, one day we expect it to rival—'

Sam put down his beer. 'Cathie, apart from occasional routine use in long-stay ICU patients, I don't have anything to do with prescribing antidepressants—'

'I'm not trying to sell it to you, Sam.' But she didn't meet his quizzical look. 'I was just building up to telling you that I saw Leslie Skinner today. She was out at Keneparu for the day. Apparently she does two days a week there. She came along to the lunch.'

'And?' He lifted one shoulder, mystified about where she could be heading. 'Is there a point to this?'

'Leslie was saying…she told me how much she enjoyed your company last Saturday night.'

'She barely saw me.' He hadn't been in the mood to party but he'd gone along to the psychiatrist's house-warming because he'd told Leslie he would. He'd spent a few hours talking with those guests he'd known, mostly the doctors among the crowd, and he'd left early. 'She was busy. There were a lot of people there.'

'A lot of people?' She looked startled. 'You mean it wasn't just you and her alone?'

'There were probably forty, maybe fifty there,' he said

impatiently. 'It was her house-warming. I didn't even know most of them.'

He saw her swallow. 'Even so, from what she was saying, it sounds as if you've been seeing quite a bit of her lately.'

Sam shrugged again. 'We've met a few times for lunch,' he said evenly. 'We've also had some professional contact through us asking her to assess unit patients.'

'We talked for quite a while after the meeting,' she said slowly, but her gaze was evasive. 'I think she must have had a free afternoon. At first I thought she was interested in our product, but as it turned out she mostly wanted to talk about you.'

She kept stopping, as if waiting for him to jump in with something, but he still had no idea where she was leading and so he said nothing. Eventually she said abruptly, 'I came away with the very strong impression that she was telling me that if I didn't want you then could I please get lost because she did.'

Sam laughed. He saw her shock at that but he couldn't help himself. It was so like Leslie. He was only surprised that she'd apparently skirted around the topic, rather than confronting Cathie directly.

'It's not bloody funny.' He'd never heard her swear before and that silenced his laughter faster than anything else could have. 'Sam, it's not funny. It was awful. What have you been telling her?'

'Nothing.' He shook his head then took a mouthful of his beer. 'At least, not much.' He laughed again. Despite seeing how much his amusement infuriated her, he couldn't help himself. 'But obviously more than I should have. Sorry.' He choked when he laughed again and she glared at him. 'I just keep imagining Leslie saying it. What did you say?'

'I didn't know what to say.' Her throat made a convulsive swallowing movement. 'I mean, what do you say to something like that?'

'Leslie's not exactly thin-skinned,' Sam pointed out, still grinning. 'She wouldn't have been bothered by you telling her to get lost.'

'I wasn't aware that I had that right any more.'

'Of course you have that right.' Bemused, he cupped her cheek. 'What am I supposed to say, Cat? Whatever I say now will be wrong. You know I don't want Leslie.'

'I'm not sure that's necessarily important to her,' she said icily. But she turned her mouth into his hand and would have kissed it if he hadn't drawn it away swiftly. 'She seems to have made up her mind that she wants you.'

'Leslie's pushing your buttons,' he observed mildly, refusing to react to the faintly pleading look she sent him. He'd make a point of having a word with Leslie, tell her to lay off, but there wasn't a lot else he could offer. 'Finding weak points has always been one of her skills. She's teasing you.'

'But she does want you.'

'Perhaps on the rebound,' he conceded. 'She's just come out of a relationship and she's feeling a bit lost. I'm familiar to her so, no doubt, I seem unthreatening. But we had our opportunity years ago and it didn't work. Nothing's changed. I like Leslie. I enjoy her company. But I'm not interested in anything more than friendship.'

'I felt sick,' Cathie said quietly. She still hadn't touched her coffee and now she pushed it away towards the window. 'I felt sick all afternoon. I couldn't even think about my work. When she talked about you coming to her house on Saturday…well, she didn't explain exactly how it was but I assumed she meant you'd spent the night together.'

'I couldn't have been there more than two hours.'

'It seemed the perfect explanation as to why you didn't care about not sleeping with me yesterday.'

Sam stiffened. 'You mean you thought I didn't want sex with you yesterday because I was already getting it somewhere else?' he asked incredulously.

'It made sense.'

'Sex,' he said hoarsely, lowering his voice when he realised that people at the next table had turned around to stare at them. 'You see, everything always comes down to sex with you.'

'It's not *just* sex,' she hissed. 'That's part of it but it's not all of it. You've obviously told her about us. I've only met her once but she seemed to know all about me. I was hurt that you'd talked about me to another woman.'

'All I said was that things were not going as well as I would have liked,' he said heavily.

'She went on and on about what a wonderful father you'd be.'

'I would try my best to be a good parent—'

'She told me she'd have your babies if I wouldn't.'

He rolled his eyes. 'She was winding you up.'

'She said you were the best lover she'd ever had.'

'She was really laying it on thick.'

Cathie sent him a withering look. 'I didn't let her get away with that one,' she said harshly. 'I said she couldn't have been around very much.'

He laughed again. Coming from Cathie, that was funny. He'd have been prepared to lay money on her having been not more than one or two partners off completely innocent when they'd first started dating. Leslie, in contrast, from his experience of having been a fellow medical student with her, had always taken an enthusiastic approach to her pursuit of sexual partners. 'Cat, you're coming back to sex again,' he warned lightly.

'I was rude to her in the end,' she said coolly.

'Leslie's not the type to bear grudges.'

'I was very jealous.'

'I suspect that was the idea.' Regardless of whatever spurious interest she nurtured in him, Leslie was still a friend. And he'd told her frankly how he felt about Cathie. He wouldn't have put it past her to try and deliberately stir up things with the vague idea of doing it to help him.

'I felt like ripping those ludicrous eyelashes right off her face.'

Sam winced. 'I'm glad you restrained yourself.'

'They're false,' she said sharply. 'I didn't mean I would have physically hurt her or anything.' He saw that the thought horrified her. 'I called you on your mobile after you left work but you didn't answer. I thought you must be with her.'

'Did you try me at home before I answered that last time?'

She nodded slowly. 'How did you know?'

'My machine was blinking to say someone had been ringing,' he told her. 'Why didn't you leave any messages?'

'Oh.' She paled. 'I've never thought about that before. I forgot that you'd be able to tell.'

He frowned, not understanding. 'You forgot…what?'

'That your machine would say that I'd called,' she said vaguely. 'I should have hung up before the bleep thing.'

'You mean you should have left your number.'

'No, I mean I should have hung up earlier,' she replied, her tone tinged with impatience now, as if she didn't know why he couldn't understand what it was she was trying to tell him. 'I shouldn't have held on so long. I shouldn't have let the bell thing chime.'

Now he was utterly mystified. 'Cathie, what are you talking about?'

She murmured something he couldn't catch. She had her elbows on the bench, her hands clasped below her chin, but abruptly she put her head down into her hands. 'This is so pathetic,' she said thickly, her voice partially muffled. 'I'm so pathetic.'

'Why?' he persisted. 'What's pathetic?'

'I listen to your machine.' She turned her head slightly so that, while it was still in her hands, two very green eyes peeked up at him. 'I call and listen to your machine.'

He blinked. 'What?'

'"Hi, this is Sam,"' she said, sitting up slowly. '"I'm not here now but leave your number and I'll get back to you."'

He still didn't understand. 'Why on earth would you want to listen to my machine? Cathie, you know you can always get the operator to bleep me at work or, after hours, I have my mobile.'

'I like hearing your message,' she murmured. 'Sometimes I just want to hear your voice. I don't need to talk to you, but I want to hear you anyway.'

'Are you mad?'

She met his sharp regard unflinchingly. 'Yes.'

He still wasn't sure he had this straight. 'So you call me at home when you know I'm not there just to listen to my voice.'

'Mmm.'

'So all those times I find the light blinking but no messages…that's you?'

She closed her eyes. 'Mostly, I expect.'

'Why haven't you ever told me this?'

'I didn't think it was important.'

'You didn't think it was important?' He could hardly believe it. 'Cathie, in two years this is the first time you've given me any indication that you think of me any time when we're not together. To me, it's always seemed as if you keep your life and me in separate filing cabinets. I've felt as if I've been excluded from all but the little corner of your world in which you keep me.' Whereas she was on

his mind, at the back of it if not at the front, all day and every day. 'I would have liked to have known that.'

'It's pretty obsessive-compulsive.'

'Oh, it's sick,' he agreed. 'In fact, you probably need help.'

'But you're flattered,' she said, her eyes widening as she made it sound like an accusation. 'You think it's great that you've turned your girlfriend into a nut case.'

'Let's just say it's not doing my ego any harm,' he admitted dryly, his pulse thudding as he registered the fact that she was still calling herself his girlfriend. 'But why did you call so much today? How did what happened with Leslie make you want to hear my voice?'

'It was strange,' she said weakly. 'I kept thinking I'd hear in your voice if you were involved with her. I kept thinking I'd be able to tell somehow. You know, half the reason I hang on so long is that I keep waiting for you to say something extra.'

'But I recorded that message more than a year ago.'

'I said it was strange,' she repeated strongly. 'I'm not claiming to be behaving rationally here, Sam.'

The idea of Cathie being irrational enchanted him. 'Is there anything else I should know about?'

'I've got a tattoo of your name on my bottom,' she said sarcastically, glaring at him with what he thought was unfair vigour when he laughed. 'You wish. No, Sam.' She leaned forward in her chair, her hands braced on his thighs, and glared right into his eyes. 'Sorry if you were expecting some other monumental revelation but the calls to your machine is as far as my madness extends at the moment.'

He lifted her hands and gave them back to her. 'Shame.'

'Although if I thought it would get you into bed I might reconsider the tattoo,' she said grimly, and he knew then that she'd understood his gesture. 'Sam, this is silly. It's been ages. I know we have some problems, I know... *I* have some problems, but we're getting there. We're talking more honestly today and yesterday than we ever have, and the way I felt when Leslie said all those things to me today has made me realise that I can't face losing you. I can't. I love you too much. If you'd just give up on this idea of settling down, everything would be perfect again.

'Sam, I want you so desperately. Let's…let's not even go back to the house. Let's get a hotel for the night and make love until dawn,' she whispered. 'Please, Sam. Feel me.' She dragged his hand to her throat and he could feel her pulse beating fast beneath his palm. 'Take me to bed.'

He drew back from her sharply, curling his hand into a fist, still feeling her against his skin although they were no longer touching. Uncomfortably aware that while his mind was strong his body had other ideas, he finished the last mouthfuls of his drink and pushed the glass to one side. He stood up. 'I meant what I said last night. No sex.'

'You're leaving me?' She sounded outraged.

'Do you have your car or do you want a lift?'

'My car's at work.'

He held out his arm to guide her outside. 'I'll walk you to it.'

They walked in silence to her office building, but in the depths of the car park she leaned back against her door, looked up at him solemnly and said quietly, 'Is this your way of blackmailing me into coming back to live with you?'

Sam sighed. He understood why she might think that, but it wasn't his intention. 'We made a mistake, going to bed so soon in the beginning,' he said heavily. 'We should have waited. I think I knew it at the time but I wanted you too much to fight it. But it was a mistake because it's meant that the sexual side of our relationship has always been so strong that it's overwhelmed everything else. It'll be good for both of us to give some time to what else we have. I believe in this, Cathie.' He kissed her cheek to say goodbye and then forced himself to resist the urge to slide his mouth across to cover her parted lips. 'Sleep well.'

'Sam!'

He'd turned away, meaning to wait at the stairwell of the car park to make sure she got away safely, but her cry brought him around before he got there.

'How long?'

'I don't know, Cathie.' He had no idea how long it would take to discover if they had anything worth salvaging. And if it didn't work, if she discovered she didn't have anything to give him beyond sex, then there was no future for them. His understanding of himself and his own needs had grown these past weeks. He couldn't go back now to allowing himself to be used like that.

'Meet me Saturday?'

'Come over to the house at lunchtime,' he agreed. He was on call on Friday night for the unit, which meant he'd finish on Saturday morning. 'I thought you said you were working?'

'I can't work like this,' she cried. 'You're driving me crazy.'

Sam smiled, hoping that she meant more than physically. 'Good,' he said softly, not meaning her to hear. 'It's your turn.'

CHAPTER NINE

LESLIE was full of laughing defensiveness when Sam confronted her in her office at Kapiti the next afternoon. 'I did it for you, Sam,' she protested. 'In fact, I was half expecting you to come dashing up here first thing this morning to kiss my feet in thanks. I thought if I dropped a few hints, those big green eyes of hers might get even greener and she might realise just what she's risking by being so awful to you.'

'A few hints?' he echoed, aghast at the understatement. 'Leslie, Cathie told me what you said.'

'Ah, well.' But she was still laughing. 'Maybe I did more than hint. But, Sam, it worked. I mean, she was trying really hard to stay polite and nice and it took a long, long time to get through to her, but by the end of my little spiel I could tell that she was absolutely livid.'

Sam frowned, puzzled. 'Cathie?' he queried. *Livid?*

'Well, a bit cross, then,' Leslie amended quickly. 'Actually, she was definitely jealous. OK, OK, so you've fallen in love with Snow White. But I did catch her glaring at me coolly once or twice.'

'She's not Snow White,' Sam said dryly. He'd have been surprised if she'd allowed Leslie to see that she'd got to her. He'd watched Cathie in operation at meetings and conferences, dealing with difficult, sometimes, to his disgust, even lecherous, medical staff, and although she'd never let him intervene in the way he'd wanted to himself he'd always been impressed with the fluid and confident way she'd handled herself.

He suspected she'd have considered it a huge breach of her professionalism to have lost her cool with one of her company's potential sales targets. Despite having met Leslie on a personal basis, the fact remained that the other woman was a consultant psychiatrist and Cathie's company was marketing an antidepressant.

'Well, anyway, she does a pretty good imitation of Snow White,' Leslie said gaily. 'I can see why you might be intrigued. Hidden heat and secret passions. Hmm, Sam?'

'Mind your own business.' He didn't mean it unkindly but he did mean it. 'No more, Leslie. No more interfering.'

'I promise.' Her grin told him he hadn't offended her. 'I'm sorry, Sam. I didn't mean to say anything, but you looked so miserable all that time she was away that when I saw her yesterday, looking so calm and contained, I couldn't resist trying to scratch some of it off to get in a dig at the real woman beneath. I didn't mean to do any harm.'

He went for the door. 'I believe you.'

'Did it help, do you think?'

'Perhaps.'

'I like her,' she said quickly. 'I suspect there's a lot of warmth there. Perhaps a lot of vulnerability, too. If only she realised that herself she'd understand how perfectly suitable she is for your protective instincts.'

'That's great,' he said dryly. 'I'm really impressed. You should think about becoming a psychiatrist.' He waved at her on his way out of the door. 'Just stop practising on Cathie or you might find yourself losing your eyelashes. Bye, Leslie.'

'Bye,' she called brightly. Then her tone changed. 'Sam? Wait! What do you mean? What do you mean, lose my eyelashes?'

He didn't think it wise to stop. Since he was on the opposite side of the hospital to ICU, closer to the maternity unit, he headed there next instead of back to the unit. He took the stairs up to the antenatal ward, wanting to look in on the woman who'd been admitted the day before with asthma. The chest physician looking after her asthma had called him an hour earlier to warn him that she wasn't improving.

'I thought I'd better mention her just in case we need to move her across to you in a hurry,' he'd explained. 'We're still hoping she's going to improve but her breathing's marginally worse this morning.'

Looking through her notes and charts before going into the room to see her himself, Sam agreed with the other doctor's opinion. When Phillipa had seen her in Casualty the day before, her peak flow—a simple measurement of how well the lungs were managing to breathe out—had been only mildly out of line with what would have been expected at her stage of pregnancy, but apart from a small improvement straight after her admission the general trend throughout the night and that day, despite treatment, had been steadily downwards.

One of the obstetric registrars had obviously seen him studying the notes because she appeared beside him. 'Hi, Dr Wheatley. She's considerably worse this morning.' The doctor sounded breathless herself. 'The medics are thinking about switching her over to intravenous bronchodilators. We'd really appreciate you seeing her.'

'Hi, Denise.' The Wellington and Kapiti obstetric services shared the same doctor-training arrangements, and because of his time covering Neonates Sam knew most of the junior doctors on the obstetric rotation. 'What's she having at the moment?'

'Four-hourly nebulised Ventolin and oral steroids,' she said, passing him the chart to show him what had been prescribed. 'Plus extra nebs when she needs them, which was just once overnight. She usually only takes an occasional Ventolin inhaler and no steroids.'

'And her baby?'

'Good heart rate, good movements. No sign of trouble there.'

'What about gases?'

'She had one set on admission and this was from this morning.' She flicked open the progress notes to show him the written results. 'These are on room air and an hour after her last nebuliser.'

Sam frowned. Her oxygen levels were acceptable but he wasn't happy with the rise in her carbon dioxide levels since admission. 'Is she on oxygen now?'

'Nasal prongs,' Denise confirmed.

'Was there an obvious trigger for this attack?'

'Nothing.' She shook her head with a firmness that suggested she'd tried hard to find one. 'No coughs or colds and she's unaware of any allergies. She got a bit wheezy for a few days in her first trimester but that settled with inhalers. Her GP didn't feel there was any need for steroids. Apart from that, for the past four or five years she's just needed an occasional puff of her inhaler in cold weather.'

'Chest X-ray?'

'From last night when she wasn't improving,' she told him as she retrieved the film from a blue X-ray envelope. She put it up on the screen. 'Basically normal, we thought.'

Sam agreed. The shield protecting the baby from the X-rays had been well positioned, but despite the baby in her abdomen compressing her lungs, he could see that there was no evidence of pneumonia.

Denise showed him to her room. 'Mrs Floyd, I'm Sam Wheatley,' he explained. Their patient was sitting bolt upright in bed, looking anxious and hot but tired as well. Her flushed face could be explained by her pregnancy, but the obvious movement of the muscles in her neck and shoulders as she puffed for breath worried him. 'I'm an anaesthetic doctor from the intensive care part of the hospital,' he added smoothly. 'One of your doctors here asked me to come and have a look at you.'

'Hello, Dr Wheatley.' She nodded. 'And, please…call me Debbie.' She was very breathless. 'Yes, Dr…Solomon told me you would be…coming to see me. It's not because…of the baby, though, is it? The…baby's fine, isn't she?'

'According to the obstetric doctors, the baby's doing just fine,' he said reassuringly. 'I'm here to see you.' He ran through a brief history while he examined her, not wanting to stress her too much by his questions but at the same time needing to be sure that nothing had been overlooked. However, she confirmed what he'd already heard from the other doctors involved in her care.

'Did you get any sleep last night?' he asked, as he drew back from listening to her chest.

'Not much.' Her smile was almost apologetic, as if she thought it had been her fault. 'I kept dropping off but…but not for very long.'

After finishing his examination, Sam explained what he thought the best course of action would be.

'She needs to come to the unit,' he told Denise when she came up to him as he was writing up the notes on the ward. 'I'm not happy with her gases and she needs an arterial line so we can monitor things more closely. I'll let my staff know and I'll speak to the medics.'

'I'll tell the nurses,' Denise said heartily, sounding relieved.

'What would your boss say to a Caesarean?'

'Her boss would say, please, let her hold on a couple of weeks,' the obstetrician said, coming up behind him, obviously having heard at least some of the conversation. 'She's not due yet. How's it going, Sam?'

'Good, James. Good.' They shook hands. 'You're not keen?'

'Not at thirty-five weeks, if I can get away without it,' the obstetrician confirmed. 'I mean, if we have to, we have to. But we're not at that stage yet, are we?'

'Not yet,' Sam conceded slowly. He understood the risks involved in an early delivery as far as the baby went, and as an anaesthetist he was fully aware of both how difficult and how dangerous it was to anaesthetise someone during an asthma attack. There was also the risk of her oxygen levels dropping at the time of inducing the anaesthetic, which meant the baby might also be deprived of oxygen at that time. However, Debbie's failure so far to respond to conventional therapy worried him. 'We'll see how she goes with the intravenous therapy.'

'You suspect she won't improve until the baby's out of there.'

'That is my concern,' Sam admitted.

'We'll keep a close eye on her while she's with you,' the other consultant said heavily. 'Have you said anything?'

Sam nodded. 'I asked how she'd feel about a Caesarean if the possibility was there, and she said she was happy to go along with whatever was best for the baby.'

'OK.' James nodded. 'I'll have a chat with her about things as well. Did I hear you say you're taking her across to your side?'

'You did,' Sam confirmed. Any of Kapiti's medical wards could have looked after Debbie's asthma, but ICU had the advantage of having staff skilled in managing both pregnancies and the arterial line he wanted to use to monitor how well her lungs were functioning.

'Good. Best place for her to be.' The obstetrician looked pleased. 'Thanks, Sam. Appreciate it. I'll rest easier tonight, knowing she's in your hands.'

The chest physician, too, was happy with his decision. 'I'll come down and see her this afternoon,' he told Sam. 'We'll keep a bed for her here on the chest ward in the hope that things improve rapidly once she's on the intra-venous therapy.'

Only Sam wasn't happy that he could call Debbie's re-sponse an improvement. 'I'd say she's stabilised at least,' Phillipa said that night as they examined her results on their evening round. 'Her peak flows are stable and her gases are better.'

'Only on higher oxygen,' Sam pointed out slowly.

'The baby's recordings are fine.'

'She's not getting any rest.' From the desk where they were standing he watched her continue to puff for breath.

He never made the decision to ventilate a patient with severe asthma lightly—technically because of the lungs be-ing so stiff and over-inflated, it was extremely difficult. In Debbie's case there was the added complication of her pregnancy, which both increased the danger of inserting the tube and, most worryingly, risked endangering the baby through a drop in her blood oxygen level.

Deciding that the fact that she was still managing, and her oxygen levels were remaining within acceptable limits while her carbon dioxide had stopped rising, didn't justify the risk of ventilating her yet, he slanted a rueful smile towards the consultant on call for the unit for the night. 'Lucy, what do you think?'

'That I wish I wasn't on tonight,' the anaesthetist said wryly. 'You'll get a panicked phone call from me in the middle of the night if I decide I need you.'

Sam smiled again. Lucy was an experienced anaesthetist and he had every confidence in both her judgement and her skills. 'I'll be on my mobile,' he promised. 'But I think she'll be fine.'

His answering machine was blinking to say there were two messages waiting for him when he arrived home. Remembering Cathie's startling confession the night before, he smiled, half expecting there to be nothing there, but this time she'd left a message.

'Sam, sorry, but I have to cancel Saturday,' she'd said, sounding as if she'd been in a hurry. 'Bye.'

But a little while later she'd obviously had second thoughts about the brevity of the message because there was another longer one from her. 'Sorry, Sam, it's me again,' she'd said faintly. 'I should have explained. Mum's in a bit of a state over this new boyfriend of hers. It sounds very confused but I think he's stolen a lot of her money. The police have been involved because she thought someone at the bank had taken the money, and now she's upset because they're chasing him, and— Oh, Sam, it's such a mess.

'I've got a vital session for work on Friday that I can't not attend but I can't get a flight until Saturday anyway. I'm going to stay with her for the weekend and try and sort things out. I really am sorry.' Then quickly, as if an afterthought, she'd added, 'I'll call you next week. I'm coming back Tuesday. Bye.'

Sam called her at home but Susan told him to try her at work, and Cathie answered on that number immediately. 'Oh, Sam.' Her voice was thick, as if she'd been crying. 'Why does she keep doing this to herself? She's only known the man three weeks but she trusted him with her ATM cards and all her details and her car keys and now he's gone, only she doesn't know if that's for ever because he's left all his clothes behind and… Sam, I don't know how to help.'

'Is this the man she went to after Harry?'

'No, a new one,' Cathie said despairingly. 'That one only lasted a few weeks. This is someone she met at the races. She thought he was quite well off and it even sounds as if she was thinking something serious might come out of it, but obviously…'

'Is there anything I can do?' Sam said gently. 'Does she need money?'

'I can give her that,' she said. 'Sam, I know you don't really want to do this, but could you just hold me for a little while?'

'I'll come and get you,' he said promptly, although her uncharacteristic plea for comfort had spun him a little off balance. He checked his watch. 'I'll be there by eight,' he said quietly. 'Are you going to have a problem getting away?'

'I'm not getting anything done here as it is,' she said huskily. 'Thanks.'

She was waiting on the street when he pulled up and she ran across and got in before he had a chance to open her door himself.

'All right?'

'Sometimes I just…well, I don't know,' she said faintly. She hugged him hard, seeming desperate for whatever comfort she could draw from him, and when she drew back her eyes were huge and wet in her pale face. 'Thank you.'

'You're welcome,' he said quietly. 'Are you coming back?'

'I'd like that, please.' She gave him a wan smile. 'Why does she keep doing this, Sam? She's forty-six, for heaven's sake. You'd think she'd have learned by now not to trust these men.' She wiped her eyes with the backs of her hands then fell back into her seat and reached slowly for the seat belt. 'She sounds absolutely beside herself and I don't know what to do. Poor Mum. I feel so helpless.'

Sam felt sorry for her but he didn't have any solution. He knew that, as always, she was feeling her mother's pain as if it were her own, only—not for the first time—he suspected that Cathie was feeling it far more strongly than Elizabeth.

His own observation was that Cathie's mother, despite

the tears and performances she went through with almost every one of her relationships, actually enjoyed her little dramas, but he doubted whether Cathie was ready to appreciate that view.

Remembering his own panicked and illogical reaction to his father's recent illness, he understood that it wasn't as easy for her to be objective about her mother's life as it was for him.

'I even tried to call Dad,' she said thickly. 'He lives so near I thought he could call around and make sure that she was all right, but he's got a locum in, covering the practice, because he's gone away on holidays. Skiing!'

Sam frowned. 'In summer?'

'France! France, Europe.' She sounded disgusted. 'Europe! With some French woman he met on his cruise to Noumea.'

'I thought he went on that cruise with…' He tried to think of her father's girlfriend's name. 'Mary, wasn't it?'

'Meredith,' Cathie supplied miserably. 'And he did. Yes. Only apparently he took one look at this girl and that was the end of poor Meredith. The locum didn't even know what this one was called but, reading between the lines, she sounds about eighteen.'

Sam hid his smile. Cathie's father was an Auckland-based surgeon with a large private practice and a reputation for being a superb clinician as well as something of a hedonist. Sam liked him. He knew he hadn't been an ideal father for Cathie but Sam had always found him sincere and open in his love for her, and the grilling the older man had subjected him to at their first meeting had reassured him that he cared very much about Cathie's welfare.

During the drive back to Sam's house she talked on about what her mother had told her and her mother's other problems and things that had gone wrong before. He stayed quiet, letting her continue while he parked and they went inside. Then he stopped her.

'Cat, you're just going round in circles,' he said gently. He drew her into his arms. 'Wait until you see her on Saturday. Things might be sorted by then or, even if they aren't, she might not be as upset by then as she sounds now.'

'But I can't stop worrying,' Cathie said faintly. 'She couldn't stop crying on the phone. I keep thinking I should go now, I should…start driving up. But the meeting on Friday's so important…' Her eyes were wet again. 'There's no one else who can cover it. It's my special project, and I've also got two learn-to-swim classes scheduled for to-morrow, but, Sam, I feel so guilty.

'I sat there tonight, wondering if I'm living my life the wrong way. I started thinking I was wrong to stay here until Friday. That leaves her alone all tomorrow and Friday. Suddenly I felt as if I was putting my job and the swimming teaching before my mother, and that started feeling wrong. What do you think? Is wanting to stay terrible? Is it? When she needs me and I'm not there for her?'

'Is anyone with her tonight?'

'One of her friends is staying.' Her chest lifted in a little hiccup as she seemed to stifle a sob. 'She's staying with Mum till next week because her apartment is being painted.'

'So she's not alone.'

'She still sounded so upset.'

'Cathie, you're her daughter.' He stroked her soft cheek. 'You're the daughter and she's the mother. And your mother has loads of friends her own age to talk this through with.' Although he considered Elizabeth's tendency to off-load her emotional ups and downs onto Cathie selfish, he'd realised long ago that it was a selfishness bred from thoughtless self-absorption rather than any deliberate wish to worry her daughter. 'You're not supposed to look after your mother,' he said softly. 'She's supposed to look after you.'

'Only it doesn't quite work like that any more.' Her expression suggested she might have liked it if it did. 'Most of the time I feel more like the mother.'

'I know you do.' Sam stroked her back. 'Cat, I imagine she'd be horrified if she knew how upset she's made you.'

There was a long silence and then she said, 'No, she wouldn't.' She lifted her forehead from where it had been resting against his chest and looked up at him. 'Oh, she would a little bit, I suppose, but part of her would be delighted.' She sighed. 'She loves all the drama.'

'Mmm.' Sam relaxed a little, hugely relieved by her sudden insight.

'You know, you're right,' she said sharply, drawing back from him. 'She has loads of friends. Loads. She's probably got a dozen with her at the moment.'

'I'm sure she has,' he said softly.

'You're a pretty smart man, aren't you, Sam Wheatley?'

'I have my moments.' He smiled. 'I take it this means you're not about to go driving off to Auckland tonight?'

'I'll stick to the plan and fly Saturday morning,' she said, more firmly now. 'Hopefully things will have settled down a little more by then.'

'I expect they will have.' Now she was no longer in need of comfort, Sam took a deliberate step back. 'Want a coffee before I take you home?'

'I'd rather have one of your omelettes.' The knowing flicker of her eyes as she took in the way he moved away from her suggested she understood why he'd ended their embrace. 'I haven't eaten since lunch.'

He put tomato in her omelette, the way she liked it, and cheese in his own and they ate in the kitchen, sitting on stools at the bench. 'This needs redoing,' she said when she'd finished her meal, tugging at a corner of the bench where the Formica was lifting. 'It's peeling right off.'

'No point.' He cleared their plates. 'I've talked to the bank and arranged the money to buy Will's house. I'm never going to have enough time to fix up this place. My solicitor's checking the mortgage contract now and then the deal's going through.'

'What?' She looked astonished. 'When did this happen?'

'Over the last few weeks.'

'But you didn't say anything.'

'You've been away,' he said mildly. 'From the way things were when you left, I assumed you wouldn't be particularly interested.'

Her lids fluttered down and she lowered her head, concealing her expression from him. 'So when will you move?'

'The tenant they had in has already left so, as far as Maggie and Will are concerned, I can have the place whenever I want,' he explained. While they'd been talking he'd made coffee and now he brought hers over to her. 'I'm on call next weekend but I thought I'd try and arrange something for either the next week or the one after.'

'But that's so soon.'

He didn't understand why she seemed shocked. It wasn't as if she hadn't known that he'd been thinking about the house. 'A couple of agents have been around here and they seem to think it'll sell fast. It's going on the market tomorrow.'

'Tomorrow?' She'd gone pale. 'But, Sam, I love this house.'

'You could buy it.'

'I've got all these plans in my head for the renovations.'

'So do them.'

'But I thought…I thought we'd do them together. Slowly. Over time.'

'Cathie, you've never told me any of this before,' he said

calmly. 'I can't read your mind and your mouth's been telling me that you don't want to live here.' He finished the last of his coffee in a few gulps and carried the mug to the sink.

'And it's too late for second thoughts. Now I've made the decision, I'm looking forward to moving.' He'd shed his shoes at the door and with his sock-covered toe he lifted a corner of the linoleum covering the floor where it, too, was lifting. 'It is falling apart but it's sound enough underneath. These floorboards would come up well with a decent sand and a polish. I hope whoever buys it cares enough about it to restore it properly.'

Then he looked up, catching her dazed look. 'Come on. Drink up. I'll drive you back to your car.'

'Take me home instead,' she said vaguely. 'I biked to work. I can take my bike home tomorrow in the car.'

Neither of them said much on the drive to her flat. He kissed her goodnight in the car, keeping the embrace deliberately light, and when he withdrew she said sharply, 'I've got swimming teaching tomorrow night and then I'll have to work on my presentation. Will I see you Friday night?'

'I'm on call.'

'I could come out to Kapiti.'

He frowned. Considering how often he'd suggested that, and how often she'd evaded his suggestions with protests about how far it was and how busy she was, her sudden urgency now worried him.

Lightly, very lightly, he cupped her cheek. 'This isn't like you, Cat. What's going on? Is it that you're still worried about your mother?'

'I don't think it's that.' But her smile was hesitant. 'I don't know, Sam. I just feel…a bit insecure, I suppose.'

'I love you.'

'You don't need me, though, do you?' She sounded flat

suddenly. 'You've just bought a house without even mentioning it to me.'

'I don't need you to survive,' he said heavily, 'but I do want you, Cat. I'm sorry you're unhappy about the house, but that was my decision. I asked you to marry me and you said no. The request is still open if you want to change your mind, but I'm not going to spend the rest of my life waiting for you to.'

'Lately, it's felt as if you're not even prepared to spend the rest of the week waiting.'

He laughed at that. He had no choice. His fiercely independent Cathie suddenly sounded a little like a grumpy child denied her favourite toy. 'Silly.' He wanted her desperately but he leaned across, opened the door and half pushed her out when at first she refused to budge. 'Home,' he ordered. 'Stop playing with my mind.'

'Happily, if you'd let me play with your body,' she mumbled, but she did, finally, get out. 'Shall I come out Friday?' She had the door almost closed, but hesitated. 'Friday night?'

'If you want. But the unit's almost full at the moment. I can't promise I won't be busy.'

'But if you're not, and if I come all that way, will you at least have sex with me?'

He laughed. 'I'll think about it.' As he drove away from her the irony of his answer made him smile again almost as much as her pleading voice had. Despite both the coolness with which he'd managed his reply and his own determination to keep his hands off her, if she did come out to the hospital he didn't see much room for doubt about where she'd be spending the night.

CHAPTER TEN

SAM'S first concern when he got to the unit on Friday morning was Debbie Floyd's asthma. The day before she'd shown no response to their treatment and he'd been worrying about her worsening overnight. However, Tim assured him that apart from a dip in her peak flow in the early hours of the morning she'd been relatively stable.

'Just no improvement,' Sam noted quietly, inspecting her chart. Debbie's peak flow was sitting around 130, well below what he would have been happy with. He looked up towards where she was resting upright against her pillows. Her breathing was still fast and laboured, every puff seeming to need all her muscles to get the air out. 'Any sleep?'

'A couple of broken episodes,' Tim told him. 'Not much at all.'

'Will, what do you think?'

'Your call, Sam.' Will sent him a sideways look. 'I'm as nervous as you are, but I'm going to be in town from eleven today so it's going to be your decision in the end.'

They went to her bed and exchanged greetings. Sam swiftly examined her. 'Essentially there hasn't been any change in three days,' he told her, replacing the stethoscope allocated to her bed on the rack at the end once he'd finished. 'You still sound very tight. Are you feeling any better at all?'

'A bit,' she puffed, but the way she didn't quite meet his gaze made him suspect she might simply be trying to please him by being appreciative of their care, rather than saying how she really felt. She reached out and touched the monitor recording her baby's heart rate. 'One-seventy,' she said breathlessly. 'She's doing very well. Dr Solomon said…as long as it's high like that…then she's fine.'

'Babies' pulse rates drop when they're unhappy,' Sam agreed. In contrast to her own pulse, which he noted was reading 126, much higher than normal. He moved back to the charts at the end of the bed and increased her steroid dose.

James Solomon came around shortly after that. Sam was seeing another patient when the obstetrician came in and he couldn't get to him before he saw Debbie, but James came over to them afterwards. 'The baby seems fine,' he told them. 'There's a good, healthy heartbeat there. She says she's still feeling pretty wheezy. How's she going?'

Sam shook his head. 'No improvement.'

'You still think we're going to have to take the baby.'

Given her lack of response to treatment, Sam didn't think there was any alternative. An early Caesarean was risky for the baby, yes, but his primary responsibility had to be Debbie. 'She's had good treatment for four days and maximum therapy for almost seventy-two hours now, with no improvement,' he reminded the surgeon. 'She's tired. If things don't turn around fast we're going to have to ventilate her. I'd say that means within the next twenty-four hours.'

'At this stage even those twenty-four hours would still make a big difference to the baby,' the other doctor said gingerly. 'I'm on call tonight and all weekend if that's any help. If there's an emergency I'm on site.'

'We'll give it a try,' Sam agreed. He had no real choice. Ultimately, when it came down to it, outside of an emergency, when he'd insist, the timing of a Caesarean was the surgeon's call. 'I'm on tonight and there's good anaesthetic cover for the weekend.'

'She still might get away without a section,' James declared, turning brisk. 'The steroids might kick in hard and she might make a dramatic turn-around. I've seen it before. I'll talk through the surgery with her and get her to sign a consent just in case, but she still might be better by the end of the weekend, giving baby another few weeks.'

'I doubt it, James.' Sam, despite his relief that the obstetrician was prepared to organise Debbie's consent for the operation, wasn't going to go as far as to agree with him. He was too aware of how easily they could lose both Debbie and the baby. 'Much as we're all hoping along with you.'

When his emergency bleeper sounded while he was in an administrative meeting late that afternoon, he ran all the way back up to the unit, fearing immediately what it signalled.

'Carbon dioxide rising,' Phillipa told him quickly. 'Ph is way down. She's dropped off a couple of times in the last five minutes.' She was tapping Debbie's cheeks. 'Wake up, Debbie. Come on, Debbie. That's good. Breathe for me. She hasn't eaten but I gave her a shot of metoclopramide.'

Sam ran his eyes down the results and nodded. The medication Phillipa had given Debbie would have helped empty her stomach and would assist in reducing the risk of her aspirating stomach contents into her lungs while he was intubating her.

He told Hine, the nurse looking after Debbie for the afternoon, what he needed, and she drew up the drugs while Phillipa explained quickly to Debbie what was going to happen. Sam retrieved the laryngoscope and a tube from the trolley.

'How's the baby?'

'One-thirty's the lowest,' Hine said tightly.

'Start printing a trace,' he instructed. 'We want a printout right through this.'

With Debbie now sedated, he lifted back her head, inserted the laryngoscope and looked at her vocal cords.

'Cricoid pressure,' he ordered as he passed the tube into her mouth, and Phillipa promptly pressed on Debbie's throat, a further measure aimed at preventing aspiration into her lungs.

'Good. That's it.' He inserted the tube smoothly, swiftly removed the 'scope, screwed on his connections and gently pumped in pure oxygen. He checked with his stethoscope that both sides of Debbie's lungs were being inflated. He'd already known Debbie's lungs would be tight, but by manually making her breathe he could feel that they were extraordinarily so. 'How's the baby?'

'Recovering,' Phillipa answered. 'One-twenty for about twenty seconds but she's up to one-forty now. One forty-eight. One fifty-two.'

'Let's get her hooked up.'

However, despite humidified oxygen and bronchodilators directly into her lungs, an hour later Debbie's lungs remained stiff. Ventilation did nothing to treat asthma, it merely removed the immediate danger of rising carbon dioxide levels. Now, given that there was still no sign of Debbie's asthma improving, Sam didn't see any alternative to a Caesarean section.

At least this time James, too, seemed resigned to the fact that they no longer had a choice. 'It certainly doesn't look as if she's going to make any recovery until the baby's out of there,' he agreed wearily, when Sam summoned him across. He worked his way through the trace they'd made of the baby's heart rate. 'There wasn't a prolonged drop when you put the tube down,' he said slowly, 'but I see what you mean by the dips now.'

'We don't have any choice with the sedation,' Sam reminded him. In order to stop Debbie fighting the machine they'd had to sedate her, despite knowing that some of the effects would leach through to the baby. 'I was hoping that the stimulation from the asthma drugs would counteract the effect of the sedation on the baby.'

'We'd better take her,' James said, his tone changing to one of briskness. He folded the trace back into shape and clipped it to the day sheet. 'I'll let Paediatrics and Theatre know. We'll aim for six. You'll be gassing, Sam?'

'I'm on for ICU tonight, not anaesthetics.' He did occasionally have a rostered night as second-on anaesthetist for Theatres but tonight wasn't one of those nights. An anaesthetic registrar, SHO and consultant would all be officially rostered to cover anaesthetics for both Theatres and Maternity. 'But I'll be there in case I'm needed.'

Tim took the call they were waiting for from Maternity about ten minutes later. 'They're ready,' he told Sam as they swiftly prepared Debbie. 'Orderlies are on their way up. And, Sam, the paeds reg just called. He wanted to ask if you could be around for the delivery in case he needs back-up. The registrar is here but his boss can't get out before seven. As Phillipa can keep things under control here, I said OK. All right?'

'I'll be there,' Sam confirmed, hoping for the baby's sake that his skills wouldn't be needed.

'Want me to do that?'

'Under control.' Sam was manually ventilating Debbie for the transfer. 'You watch the monitors. Hine's doing the drips.' He looked up quickly and signalled to Phillipa, who was talking with some relatives over the other side of the unit, to warn her that they were on their way.

As they were coming out of the unit Sam saw that Cathie was waiting to one side, as if about to go in. 'Cat!' He'd forgotten she'd said she was coming out, but he couldn't stop now and he called for her to follow them. 'Come this way.'

'You're busy,' she said faintly, but she hurried to catch

up with them. 'Sorry. I should have called. Where should I wait?'

'Hine, can you reach the keys in this pocket and chuck them to Cathie?' He needed both hands to ventilate Debbie, but he positioned himself so that the nurse could retrieve the keys from the pocket of his white coat. 'Cat, take these. Go back to the unit and ask Phillipa, my registrar, to explain where the flat is. I'll call you when I know what's happening.'

As they were almost at the lift designated for ICU and Theatre use only, there wasn't time for anything else, but Cathie's hesitant smile seemed to suggest that she didn't mind.

Main Theatres were in the same block as the unit, but Caesareans were performed in one of the newly opened theatres in the obstetric block, meaning they had to go down to the second level and across the internal bridge connecting the buildings.

Two midwives were waiting at the entrance to the wing to escort them, and Hine handed over Debbie's details to them while they all moved swiftly towards the theatre suite.

Sam had already briefed both the anaesthetist on call and the anaesthetic registrar by phone, and they exchanged greetings. An anaesthetic technician took over the bagging while Sam helped set them up then went to change. Glancing into Theatre from the anaesthetic room, he'd seen that the surgical team was already scrubbed and waiting. When he got back Debbie's abdomen had been painted with iodine solution and every other part of her was being draped with sterile green guards.

He went to see if everything was ready for the baby. 'All set,' the paediatric registrar said quietly, standing back so that Sam could see the incubator and the resuscitation table beneath the radiant heater, which would supply the heat the baby would need. There was a full range of resuscitation equipment, including suction, airways, masks and a paediatric laryngoscope, used for examining the airway and for inserting any of the tiny tracheal tubes which were laid out beside it.

What he wanted most to see was vials containing the antidote to the sedating pain relief Debbie was being given, and he saw that there were two of them waiting, along with an ampoule of vitamin K which they routinely administered to babies at Kapiti as soon as they were born.

'Thanks, Dr Wheatley,' the younger doctor said. 'Hopefully you won't be needed, but thanks for coming.'

'No problem.' Sam pulled on gloves. He didn't mind staying. The registrar was relatively junior and he was happy to be there to supervise. Besides, being in Theatre was far easier on his nerves than waiting in the unit for an emergency call. Even without Debbie's asthma, the delivery would have been relatively high risk since it involved a general anaesthetic for the mother.

Sam saw James start to draw a scalpel across the lowest part of Debbie's abdomen, and his eyes went immediately to the anaesthetic machine and then to the machine monitoring Debbie's recordings. Her pulse was up to 130 and her systolic pressure was dropping. It was at 100, down from 110 a few minutes earlier. The duty anaesthetist lifted his brows at Sam above his mask and then said quietly to James, 'Make it fast.'

'Almost there,' the obstetrician said tightly. 'Less than five.' With the help of his registrar, Sam saw that he'd retracted Debbie's skin and stomach muscles and was beginning on the uterus. Sam noted the expert way he manipulated the scalpel, making multiple thin, fine but swift cuts, designed to protect the baby underneath, rather than risking one deeper incision.

'Suction,' James ordered, as he entered the uterus and cut the sac. 'Meconium, Sam. I'd say moderate.'

'OK.' Sam saw that the paediatric registrar had noted that as well. Meconium staining of the amniotic fluid was a sign that the baby had been in distress, and it meant that there was a risk that she might have aspirated some of the contaminated fluid into her lungs.

'She's flat.' The obstetrician and his assistant had suctioned the baby's mouth and nose as he'd delivered her, and now he lifted the infant out and handed her to one of the midwives who was waiting with a warm towel to collect her. 'Start the clock. She's not breathing.'

Sam moved to help. While the paediatric registrar went for one tiny arm to get venous access, Sam carefully inserted the paediatric laryngoscope and inspected her airways. Despite meconium having contaminated the amniotic fluid, there was no sign of any in her airways so he smoothly withdrew the scope and gently ventilated her using a mask and bag, watching the gentle rise and fall of her chest to confirm that the oxygen was reaching her lungs.

His fingers automatically checking the side of her neck, he felt a good pulse. 'How's the monitor going?'

'Connecting now.' The midwife, moving fast, pressed on the final lead and Sam saw that the infant's heart rhythm was normal. While it was slower than he'd have preferred, it was above his threshold for alarm at 100.

'I'm giving one mil of naloxone,' the registrar said as he injected the dose slowly into the cannula he'd inserted into a vein in the baby's hand.

Sam nodded, agreeing with the dose as the baby was clearly over two kilos. The naloxone would act as an antidote to the opiate Debbie was being given to relieve the pain of the surgery.

'Breathe, baby. Breathe,' the midwife whispered beside him.

Sam sent her a quick look, intended to be reassuring, as he continued to pump small puffs of oxygen into the infant's lungs. He wasn't overly concerned yet by the baby's slowness to respond. He spared a glance at the large clock above his head. While the time to him had seemed to pass very slowly, it wasn't yet two minutes since she'd been delivered. In another two he might start to worry, but not yet.

She was clear of meconium, her heart rate was rising fast and the pain relief and sedation Debbie had been given meant he was still prepared to put her failure to breathe down to respiratory depression from the opiate.

A few seconds later, as the naloxone took abrupt effect, he felt resistance against the bag and the baby opened big blue eyes, curled her fists and took an independent breath. 'Good girl.' Sam waited for her to take a few more breaths, then smoothly removed the mask and held it above her nose and wailing mouth.

'She's fine,' he told James, too busy to turn around to look at him, although he felt the relaxation of tension in the Theatre as if it were a tangible thing. 'How's Debbie?'

'Holding,' the anaesthetist came back swiftly. 'Just. Systolic still 100. James, you almost done?'

'Closing the uterus now,' the surgeon confirmed.

The paediatric registrar finished fastening the line he'd used into place with tape and a splint made, Sam saw—no doubt as some reflection of budgetary restraints at Kapiti— from taped tongue depressors. 'Thanks, Dr Wheatley. I can finish up here if you like. I'll take her through to Special Care. The boss should be arriving any minute and he'll take a good look at her. Will her mother be able to feed?'

'Definitely not tonight.' He wouldn't be attempting to wean Debbie from the ventilator until there were strong signs of improvement in her asthma, and that could take days. 'We had to intubate her tonight when she almost arrested.'

Leaving the baby in the hands of the midwife and the

other doctor, Sam wrote up the notes then turned his attention back to Debbie. James was just finishing, swiftly sewing up the wound with a long, neat, subcutaneous suture.

'Thanks, Sam.' The obstetrician glanced his way. 'I presume she'll be with you for a day or two yet.'

'Hopefully not much longer than that,' Sam agreed.

'She's still very tight.' His colleague passed him the earpieces of his stethoscope to use, and Sam listened at either side of her lungs, confirming that there was still widespread wheeze.

Tim and Hine came across to help with Debbie's transfer back to the unit, and by the time he had her back in place and settled enough for him to be able to spare a few minutes to run over to see Cathie it was after nine.

'Cat, I'm sorry,' he said, gathering her into his arms for a quick hug when she answered the door. 'It's been a difficult night and we're expecting another two admissions. I might not get away again. Are you all right?'

'Fine.' She smiled. 'You did warn me you might be busy. I don't mind.' She held up a copy of the Australian and New Zealand *Anaesthesia and Intensive Care Journal.* 'I've been reading.'

'Sorry. It's probably the only thing here there is to do. I keep meaning to buy a little television or a radio.'

'How is that lady you were with? Has she had her baby? Was that where you were taking her?'

'She had a baby girl.' Keeping his arm around her, he guided her back into the main living area of the townhouse. 'Premature, but she seems fine.' Cathie had brought an overnight bag and it was sitting on the floor against the wall, still zipped up. 'Cat, are you sure you want to stay? You might be wasting your time. I can't guarantee that things are going to settle down. I won't be offended if you want to go back into town.'

'I want to stay. I don't have to be at the airport until ten tomorrow morning and I've brought all my things so I can drive straight there. Have you eaten?'

'Not yet.' Tim had saved him a meal from the ones delivered from the kitchen but he hadn't had a chance to get to it.

'Have you got ten minutes to spare for a picnic?'

'Five,' he conceded. He followed her into the kitchen, expecting her at most to have picked up perhaps some chocolate or bags of chips for them, but to his amazement she retrieved a beautifully displayed platter of pâté and cheeses and grapes from the small fridge in the corner, along with a stick of French bread. 'This looks wonderful.'

'There were chicken drumsticks, too, but I got hungry, waiting,' she said lightly, passing him a hospital-issue plate from one of the cupboards. 'Sorry. There's chocolate mousse for dessert. Are you allowed wine?'

'I'll stick to cola.' He had some cans in the fridge and he fetched one. 'Cat, this is very…thoughtful. Thank you.'

'You used to make picnics for me all the time,' she said quietly, as they ate. 'Whenever I had to go into work at the weekends, if you were free you'd bring me lunch. Do you remember?'

'I remember you telling me to stop.' He spread a layer of brandy-scented pâté over his bread, waiting until he'd finished it, as well as some cheese, before adding, 'I remember you deciding that me interrupting you was too much of a distraction and I remember being banned from your office.'

'That wasn't because of the food,' she protested, her eyes widening. 'It was because you always insisted on taking off my clothes before you'd let me eat.'

Sam shrugged. 'The best picnics are eaten naked.'

'We could take off our clothes now.'

'Not if you don't want me to lose my job.' Smiling, he held her chin with one hand and wiped her crumb-speckled mouth, using a napkin, with the other, before kissing her. 'As unbearably tempting as that suggestion sounds, Cat, I have to go.'

'I'll leave everything in the fridge in case you're hungry when you finish,' she said quickly, scrambling up to follow him out to the door. 'Sam, if I'm asleep when you get back, wake me up, won't you?'

'See you soon.' He kissed her again, swiftly this time, his mind already shifting back to his work.

It was, however, after three before he got back to the flat. Cathie had left the door unlocked and the lights on downstairs for him, but she was deeply asleep in his bedroom upstairs and he took care not to wake her.

He got up just after six, took a quick shower and dressed. As she was still sleeping, he set the alarm beside the bed to ring at eight so it would wake her in plenty of time for her to get to the airport. He left her a note, thanking her for the food and hoping that things went well with her mother.

Debbie Floyd was starting to respond to treatment. By lunchtime when he left, her chest had loosened considerably. That improvement continued over the weekend, and on Monday afternoon he gave the order to remove her tube.

She was still wheezy but her blood gases stayed good and her peak flow continued to rise slowly. After a couple of hours he agreed that it was safe for Hine to take her across to the special care unit to see her daughter.

The nurses in Special Care had taken photographs and made a short video of the baby for her, which they'd all watched about a dozen times, but because of the risk of exposing the baby to hospital infections it hadn't been possible to bring her over to the unit to meet her mother.

'I'm so excited, Dr Wheatley.' Despite her breathlessness and wheezing and the discomfort she must have been in from her Caesarean wound, she was managing to bounce around in her bed while they waited for the orderlies to arrive to help with her transfer. 'I can't believe it. I'm going to see her. I still can't believe it. I can't believe I've even had her yet. She looks so beautiful on the video.'

'She's even more beautiful in real life,' Sam assured her with a smile. He'd checked on the baby that morning and, aside from needing some light therapy to treat mild jaundice—not unexpected because of her prematurity—she was doing very well.

Given that the severity of Debbie's asthma attack meant that after they discharged her from the unit, probably the next day, she'd need to spend at least the rest of the week on one of the medical wards, he thought there was every chance that mother and baby would be ready to leave hospital at the same time.

Tim came up to the main station a short while later as Sam was reading through the notes on a transfer he'd accepted from Palmerston North that morning. 'Every woman in this place is turning clucky,' the charge nurse grumbled. 'If this keeps up I'm going to have to call more staff in for this afternoon just to cover for the ones who keep dashing off to Special Care to peep at the baby. You know Prue *and* Hine *and* Phillipa have all gone down with Debbie now.'

'Phillipa?' Sam lifted his brows. 'But Phillipa isn't interested in babies.'

Tim rolled his eyes. 'She said she thought she'd best go in case Debbie has a relapse with the excitement. She took a 'scope and tube with her but that was just for show. I suspect young Phillipa is having second thoughts about not wanting babies. She's always carrying on about not wanting the labour pain, but now she's seen how Debbie's got through it without any pain she's getting thoughtful. You wait. Tomorrow she'll be asking you if you'd be prepared to give her a general anaesthetic if she asks nicely and gives you nine months' notice.'

Sam laughed. 'I'll tell her that if she has a respiratory arrest and nearly dies on us just before the baby's due, I'll be happy to. Have you been over to see the baby, Tim?'

'Twice.' The nurse pulled a rueful face. 'OK. OK. I'm as bad as the rest of them. What about you?'

'Once this morning and once on Saturday,' Sam admitted, adding lightly, 'On a professional basis, of course.'

'Oh, yeah, Sam.' Tim's grin suggested he saw through him. 'Just because they've got a whole team of paediatric doctors and nurses, it doesn't mean they can manage on their own over there.'

'She is cute,' Sam conceded.

'So you're just as clucky as the rest of us.' Tim laughed. 'I guess we're all getting to that age. Well, at least to the age that we'd better hurry up and make up our minds before we're too old for it. So, are you and Cathie…?' At Sam's quizzical look, he grinned. 'We saw her the other night,' Tim reminded him, 'when she came to meet you as we were taking Debbie across to Theatre. And let me just say that having met her, however briefly, I understand completely why you weren't tempted by our determined psychiatrist,' he added lightly.

When Sam merely returned his open look with calm silence, Tim grinned. 'And it's none of my business,' he agreed. 'I'll take some stickies,' he said, tugging the labels free of the notes Sam had been reading. 'For the patient's MRSA swabs. Is Phillipa going to change his lines?'

'I'll come and start in a few minutes,' Sam told him. 'Phillipa's obviously tied up, supervising Debbie.'

All transfers from other hospitals were nursed in one of the side rooms if they had one spare until their MRSA swabs—a way of checking for the presence of an antibiotic-resistant and contagious staphylococci bacteria—were shown to be negative. Once the staphylococci became established within an intensive care unit it was difficult to eradicate and there was a risk of other patients becoming infected.

As well as taking the swabs, unit protocol dictated that they routinely changed all indwelling lines and catheters because they might also be harbouring contamination.

He had hoped to get out to the airport that evening to meet Cathie off her flight from Auckland but, with the unit being full now, they were busy and he was several hours too late getting away from the hospital.

Cathie had called him each night she'd been away. That surprised him because she'd never done anything like that before. Normally when she went away he heard nothing until she arrived back—he hoped that didn't mean that the time with her mother had been more traumatic for her than she'd made it sound.

He called her as soon as he got home but Susan told him she'd gone to the gym and then to teach a swim class. 'Sam, she said she might not be home tonight so she's probably planning on calling on you later.'

Leaving a note on his door in case they missed each other and she came to the house, Sam headed down to the pool. He could see her teaching a small group of nervous-looking teenagers at the far side of the pool when he emerged from the changing area. He asked one of the lifeguards to let Cathie know he was in the pool when she finished her class, then dived into one of the lap lanes himself and began swimming fast lengths.

He'd done two kilometres by the time she grabbed his legs. She indicated the other side of the pool and they both ducked down and swam across the bottom beneath the swimmers doing lengths in the next three lanes.

She was laughing when he surfaced. 'You looked like you were in a race,' she said accusingly. 'You were going so fast you'd frightened the rest of them out of the lane. I was almost too scared to interrupt you.'

'Perhaps I was working off my...physical tensions,' he said ruefully, still breathing hard from the exertion of his swim. He shook his head free of water then held out his arms and she swam into them. 'Hello.' He kissed her. 'How was it?'

'Much better than I was expecting.' Her hands clutched at his shoulders and she twined her legs around his thighs. 'You were right as usual. Underneath all the drama she wasn't too bad. The police found her car dumped way up north somewhere. They don't hold out much hope about the money, but it turns out he didn't get as much as she thought he had so she's going to be all right. Yesterday she even started talking about some guy who's just moved in upstairs from her.'

Sam grinned. A few strands of dark hair had come loose from Cathie's swimming cap and he tucked them back in. 'Your mother's never going to change.'

'I asked her why this morning. I asked her why, when men had made her so unhappy so many times, couldn't she just accept that she might be better off on her own.'

'And?' He kissed her chlorine-scented nose.

'She told me that I thought too much,' she said flatly.

Sam laughed. 'Well, you know I think that, too,' he said easily.

They swam back to the side of the pool. 'She fancies you, of course.'

Sam had, from time to time, wondered about the enthusiasm of her mother's kisses. 'I'm in love with her daughter.'

Cathie spread her arms along the ledge just above the water and kicked out from the side so that her body floated, her legs on either side of his. 'Sam, I've been doing a lot of thinking this weekend and I...' Her voice faded and he saw her bite into her lower lip as if she was nervous. When she spoke again the words came rushing out. 'Sam, if it's really that important to you, I'm prepared to go through with what you want and marry you.'

Sam froze. His feet stopped kicking and his head dropped momentarily beneath the surface. Then he kicked himself off from the bottom of the pool and came up next to her, mimicking the way she supported herself to float beside her.

'Does that mean yes or no?' she asked faintly.

'It means...I don't know.' He didn't look at her. 'Why, Cathie? Why now?'

'Why?' She looked puzzled. 'Because I love you.'

'You loved me two months ago,' he pointed out gently, 'but when I asked you to marry me then you didn't hesitate to say no. And last week you told me you couldn't live with me. Loving me wasn't enough for you then. What's changed now?'

'Seeing Mum, perhaps. Thinking about how happy she is when she's happy, and the way you made me realise that she's not as miserable as I've always thought she was when her relationships ended. I've been thinking that perhaps I should grab for happiness when I can get it. Even if I know our marriage might not work out in the long term, we can be happy for a little while at least. And it's what you want, isn't it?'

'A little while?' Sam felt sick. 'Cathie—'

'Sam, I don't want to lose you. If marriage is what it takes to keep you, I'll do that. I'll marry you.'

His head was spinning. 'Because otherwise you'll lose me?'

'It feels like I'm on the verge of doing that,' she said faintly. 'Lately it's felt as if you're...slipping through my fingers somehow. I don't want that to happen.'

'Cathie, you're nothing like your mother,' he said

hoarsely. 'Or your father. Nothing at all. And neither am I. Just because their marriages fail, it doesn't mean that will ever happen to us.'

Despite the warmth of the water, he saw goose-bumps form on her shoulders and arms and she sank lower so that the water lapped her chin. 'Is this another part of you playing hard to get or have you changed your mind about wanting me?'

'I haven't changed my mind.' He supposed he deserved the first part of the comment. 'And I'm not meaning to play hard to get,' he added. In fact, the panicked insecurity of her reaction to that had alarmed him when he'd realised that it was only happening because she thought he was withdrawing from her. 'I realise that it must look like that,' he said slowly, 'but, by taking away the sex, I wasn't trying to distance myself from you. I'm simply trying to refocus our relationship.'

'I feel very distant from you at this moment,' she said faintly.

'I'm sorry.' Sam didn't know what else to say.

'You don't want to marry me any more.'

'Not like this,' he said heavily. He wanted her to marry him because she was as intoxicated with love for him as his love for her intoxicated him. He didn't want it to be out of capitulation to some emotionally manipulative game he'd inadvertently created. And he certainly couldn't go through with it, knowing she expected them to divorce eventually.

The realisation that perhaps he wanted too much and too greedily turned him cold.

'Tell me what you want me to say,' she whispered, and he saw that her face had gone pale. She let go of the pool's side and came around to face him, digging her fingers into his shoulders. 'Sam…? Sam, I thought I was offering everything you wanted now. What's wrong? Whatever you want me to say, I'll say it. Just tell me. Please.'

He still felt sick. 'Cathie, that's not how it's supposed to work.'

'So, now I've finally given in to you, you're rejecting me?'

'I'm not rejecting you,' he said thickly. That she could describe her proposal as having *given in* to him confirmed all his worst fears. 'We need…time.' The sensible part of him said that he should end it now, that she was never going to feel the same way as he did and that stopping it here would shorten the pain for both of them. The sensible part of him said that he should do that now, but the rest of him wasn't that strong.

'I'll call you,' he said grimly, not being meaning to be vague or cruel but nowhere near being able to consider how long it was going to take to come to terms with what the future held for them.

Not looking at her, he turned to the wall and heaved himself out of the pool to get himself away from her before she could see how much leaving her was costing him.

CHAPTER ELEVEN

SEVERAL of Sam's friends had offered to help him with the move to Will's house but Sam had decided it would be easier to hire professionals. Strangely, it still felt like Will's house even once he had his furniture installed.

'It'll only be like that for a week or two,' Maggie assured him, strolling around the timber-floored living area. They'd come to visit him on his first weekend in the house. 'Once you buy a bit more furniture and unpack and get a few pictures up it'll feel more like yours.'

He liked the house. Set high on a hill on a large leafy section, the views of Wellington's harbour were compelling and magnificent. He liked watching the changing colours of the water and the sky, and after the bustle of Newtown he liked the tranquillity.

'What does Cathie think?' Will asked calmly. 'Is she relieved we persuaded you out of the dump at last?'

Sam turned around from the window in time to catch an exasperated look passing from Maggie to her husband. 'Cathie and I are having a break,' he said slowly. 'Whether that's going to be temporary or permanent is still unclear.'

'Sam, I'm sorry.' Maggie rolled expressive eyes in the direction of Will, as if to apologise for his question. 'I'm sorry you two are still having problems, but it's none of our business.'

The last words were very clearly directed at Will, but the other man merely grinned. 'Sam's a big boy,' he said easily. 'And they're perfect for each other. He'll work it out.'

Sam wished he shared Will's confidence. It had been

more than two weeks since the afternoon he'd left Cathie in the pool, and as he was no nearer to knowing what he was going to do now than he had been then he still hadn't contacted her. He'd had some vague idea that time would help him see things more clearly but all time seemed to be doing was making life without her seem all the more deficient.

He understood that her upbringing might have made her think that marriage was a temporary, invariably painful thing, but if loving her the way he had these past two years hadn't given her enough of a sense of security to overcome her fears what chance did he have of changing her opinion now?

If he gave in to the weak part of himself, the part that wanted to snatch her up and hold her tight, then his life would be hell, wouldn't it? Knowing that she was marrying him not out of love but out of desire and the fear of losing him, wasn't he setting up a marriage guaranteed to fail just as surely as she'd be expecting it to?

He saw the notice about the meeting her company was sponsoring on a notice-board at the hospital at the beginning of the following week. He spent the next four days telling himself that there was no need for him to attend any session about an antidepressant and that in all probability some rep other than Cathie would be giving the talk, but he still found himself outside the seminar room in the hospital's small post-graduate centre at lunchtime on Friday afternoon.

'Sam!' Leslie, accompanied by a huddle of psychiatrists-in-training, fluttered her lashes at him as she came up, threw the door open and swept him along with her juniors into the room. 'Good to see you. Are you really interested in this, or like me, have you come for Cathie and the free lunch?'

'Lunch,' said Sam, automatically taking the paper plate

she thrust into his hand before guiding him towards a large array of sandwiches and muffins. His heart was thumping. 'Is Cathie doing the session?'

'Oh, yes.' Leslie, falling into the queue around the food, started sorting through the sandwiches. 'Can you see any without meat? Didn't she tell you?'

'I wasn't sure.' He passed her a tray containing egg and salad sandwiches.

'Cathie and that good-looking guy she works with. They seem to be doing these sessions together lately. Mark, is it?'

'Martin.' Sam gritted his teeth. He chose sandwiches and a muffin at random, accepted the juice Leslie offered and found himself a seat in the back row of the fifty or so chairs that had been laid out in front of the whiteboard and lectern.

Leslie plonked herself next to him and started chatting about this and that, but he barely registered her presence. The room was filling up and there was quite a bit of noise. Then Cathie came in, carrying a big tea-kettle, and the rest of the room seemed to fade out.

She looked paler than usual, a little flustered even, which for her meant a vague air of distraction when normally in her work she was so controlled. Then she put the kettle down, turned to the audience and saw him. He felt the connection like an electric shock.

He saw first colour flood up above the collar of the white blouse she was wearing but then the colour faded as fast as it had come, leaving her paler than ever.

She didn't smile or nod or acknowledge him in any way but, then, she didn't need to any more than he did. He felt her awareness of him as intently as he felt his own of her.

'Cathie isn't looking very well,' Leslie whispered beside him. 'Quite peaky, in fact. She's not pregnant, is she, Sam?'

Sam choked. He managed a rough denial but then had to gulp his juice to calm his throat. 'No,' he said again, more clearly once he had his breath back. Or, at least, if she was, it wasn't by him.

The thought made him grit his teeth again, and when Martin sauntered in after Cathie, carrying a tray with milk and sugar, he had trouble restraining himself from snarling at the other man.

'Coffee?' Leslie asked, hopping up, obviously intent on joining the small queue forming at the drinks. 'Or tea?'

Sam shook his head stiffly. His hands were shaking and he wasn't about to trust himself with any liquid.

It was more than a year since he'd attended one of Cathie's presentations, but he was used to her being a fluid and confident speaker who made whatever she was talking about sound interesting and compelling. Today, though, just the sensation of being in the same room with her, like that first time they'd met, was so overwhelming that Sam could no more have listened to her than flown a plane.

He was dimly aware of her voice, but not her words, and he just watched her, thought about her and them and everything there'd been between them, and ached for her.

The first inkling he had that things might not be going as smoothly as usual for her came when Leslie nudged him with her elbow. 'She really isn't well,' she hissed. 'Sam, she's going pink then pale, pink then pale, and she's hardly making any sense. Perhaps you should take her home.'

Sam frowned. It seemed that Martin, too, from the way he was watching Cathie, had noticed something amiss because he stood suddenly and took over.

'However, it's the *rise* in the levels of serotonin between the ends of the nerves which our product has been associated with that is the most significant feature,' he said smoothly, the subtle emphasis on the word 'rise,' along with the pointed look he shot Cathie, suggesting that she might have mistakenly said the opposite.

But Cathie's vague look in reply seemed to indicate that

she either didn't realise or didn't care. She sat down, though, as if the change-over in presenters had been a planned manoeuvre, and she crossed her legs and looked at the floor.

Martin droned on but Sam couldn't look away from Cathie. When she eventually lifted her head she seemed to be taking care to look anywhere but at him, but he didn't take his eyes away and finally, finally, she met his regard. He saw her flinch as if it had hurt her, and she looked abruptly away again.

'Cathie!' Martin's strident command drew Sam's gaze even if it hadn't Cathie's. 'Cathie?'

'Hmm?' She looked up quickly, her clouded gaze suggesting she'd forgotten where she was. 'Sorry?'

'The tape,' Martin said strongly. 'The tape from the symposium? Doctors, this is a three-minute excerpt of Professor Simpson's concluding remarks about our product from the symposium. I think you'll find it interesting.'

Leslie bumped him with her elbow again. 'Sam, look at her. Do something. I've never seen her like this before. She can't be well at all.'

Sam didn't know what he could do. He understood that his presence there had flustered her but seeing her had done the same to him, and even when they'd been together properly she wouldn't have appreciated him intervening in anything to do with her work.

She seemed to be getting herself back together. While she'd fumbled about when trying to find what looked like the small tape player Martin was asking for, once she had it and had passed it to him she sat down again looking marginally more confident.

'She's all right now,' he told Leslie.

Martin repeated the significance of the tape they were about to hear, then he held it up towards them and pressed a button.

'Hello, this is Sam.' Sam froze. He met Cathie's panic-stricken look with silent incredulity. The fact that he'd said 'hello' instead of 'hi' told him that this was the new message, the one he'd recorded after moving to the house, not the old one from Newtown. She'd called him at the new house?

He felt Leslie stiffen beside him, as if she'd recognised the strangeness of what she was hearing, but everyone still seemed to be waiting expectantly for some discourse on the properties of the antidepressant being promoted. Instead of that, his own voice went on, 'I'm out so please leave a message after the bleep.'

Only there wasn't any bleep. There was just silence and then a few murmurs from the audience. The message started to repeat itself. Someone laughed. A few people chuckled.

Martin seemed to be taking a while to understand why he hadn't just heard the speech he'd been expecting to hear, but then he managed a sort of smile. 'I…think…well, obviously that was the wrong tape,' he said unevenly, moving quickly to shut off the sound of Sam's voice. 'But perhaps my colleague has the right one somewhere?'

Cathie looked numb. Then she moved suddenly and retrieved another tape from her handbag and passed it to Martin. But before he could start it she walked forward a little.

Sam felt as if their eyes were glued together. 'What do you want me to do?' she said clearly, talking to him as if they were alone in the big room instead of surrounded by at least thirty startled doctors. 'Do you want me to quit?'

'I've never said I wanted that,' Sam said heavily.

'Would it make a difference?'

'I don't want you to quit.'

'Is it the hours? Do you want me to cut down on the hours? Or is it the travel?'

'It's not your job,' he said calmly into the enthralled silence surrounding them. 'It's never been your job.'

'Is it children? We can have children, Sam. I love children.'

'Cat, it's nothing to do with children or work.'

Beside him Leslie stood abruptly and then urged him to his feet. 'How about you two sort this out outside?' she said cheerfully. 'Come on, Sam. Cathie, you, too. Come on. Outside. We haven't all come along here to hear about your romance. We want to hear about antidepressants.'

There were loud choruses of complaint at that, suggesting that Leslie might have misread the mood of her colleagues, but Sam let her steer him out. She returned a few seconds later with Cathie. Leslie pushed her out towards him then pulled the door firmly closed behind them.

Sam took Cathie's cold hand and led her outside into the sun to a bench on the grass in front of the building. 'When did you call?' he demanded huskily. 'The light hasn't been blinking.' Since she'd told him about her anonymous calls he hadn't had a single one.

'I hang up now before the tone,' she said weakly. 'Sam—'

'Cathie—'

They both spoke at the same time then stopped, but he waved her to continue.

'I'm going to lose my job,' she said weakly. 'After that. There'll be complaints. Martin will complain even if none of the audience does.'

Sam smiled. 'Speaking as an objective member of the audience, no one will complain,' he replied. 'Those doctors are only there for the food. Any extra excitement is a definite bonus. And if the weasel wants to complain he'll have me to answer to. Tell him that and scare him off.'

'He's not a weasel,' she protested, though it seemed like an automatic response and not a very determined protest.

'Actually, I wouldn't mind that much if I did lose the job. I haven't been that enthusiastic about it lately. I've been thinking that I do an awful lot of work for something that isn't really that important to the world. I could take a job as a lifesaver or go back into nursing.'

'Your enthusiasm will come back.' He stroked her hair. 'I have to say I've been a bit distracted myself these past weeks.'

'I was even thinking about how nice it would be to have a break for a few years and have babies.'

Sam couldn't stop touching her. He slid his finger across her cheek, brushed her chin, stroked her throat. 'Go on.'

But she didn't. She sighed, then dropped her eyes. 'How's the new house?'

'Good. Come and visit me.'

'I'd like that.' But she looked uncertain. 'If I thought you wanted me to. But I don't know these days. I don't know much at all. Sam, you've turned me into a nervous wreck. Why are you punishing me like this?'

'I'm not punishing you, Cat.' Not deliberately. He sighed. 'At least not any more than I've been punishing myself. I need time to decide whether I'm ready to compromise yet with you. It's not an easy decision to come to and I don't know if I'm there yet. I still want to have it all.'

He touched her hair where she held it bunched at her neck with a clip, marvelling at its soft smoothness. 'I understand objectively that I can't but that doesn't stop me still wanting everything.'

'But I want to give you everything.' She sounded so desperate he almost believed her. 'I am yours, Sam. Completely. I didn't realise how completely until you took yourself away. I barely know what to do with myself without you. It's as if my brain is set on automatic and I go through the days the way I should be going through them, but there's no sparkle any more. There's no excitement. I feel as if I don't have anything to look forward to. I don't want to it to be like this. Sam, I need you. Please. Tell me what it is you want me to say.'

'You're just about…getting there,' he said thickly. He could hardly think. His heart pounding, he pulled her into his arms and held her trembling body tight. 'Cat, it has never been your job, or you not wanting children.' He spoke harshly, roughly almost, into her hair, desperate for her to understand.

'That's all superficial stuff. I want to have children with you and for us to bring them up together, but that's something you also have to want passionately for it to happen. I don't want to change you or stop you working, but if you want to do something different then I'll support you through that. I want us to be equal, Cat. I want us to be equal in our love. I don't want to be the one who's always on the outside, looking in at you and wanting you so much but always knowing that you were keeping some secret part of yourself aloof. I want marriage to be what you want, but most of all I want you to believe it will last for ever because I can't handle any commitment less than that.'

'Sam—'

'Shh. Let me finish.' He released her a little, but put her hand across her mouth to still her. 'I want you to marry me for no other reason but that you can't not let me share your life.'

'That's what I want,' she said faintly.

'But every other time we've talked about marriage you've been so sure it wouldn't work. After less than a month at the house you were talking as if it had been a disaster.'

'That was because I kept thinking it was going to be,' she whispered. 'I could never relax because I thought our feelings would slip away if we did.' She touched his cheek.

'Sam, please try and understand. I've seen so many divorces and misery and unhappy people—I don't mean just Mum and Dad, but friends and some of the kids I teach swimming to, as well as the homeless ones I've met through the charity—so that to me it felt like our love was something extraordinarily precious. I've always been frightened of losing that. I've always thought that if we tried to capture our love, if we tried to make it a conventional thing the way everybody else does, then we'd lose it. I didn't want to toy with perfection.'

'But now you're willing to do that?'

'I can't not,' she said faintly. 'Sam, I have to. We have to. You've got me in such a state that I can't think rationally any more. You heard that tape. I'm a nut case. I've recorded you so many times you fill the tape and I play it to myself about a hundred times a day.' She swallowed heavily. 'I used to try so hard to keep things light, to pretend that I was in control so that I wouldn't be hurt when things went wrong. But I don't care any more. I'm prepared to risk anything now just for us to be together again. I love you, Sam. I want to be with you for the rest of my life. Please, tell me you want that, too.'

'I want to hear more,' he said softly. 'Tell me how much you love me again.'

'Well…' But then she stopped. 'You ghastly, horrible, awful, manipulative man,' she stormed, her eyes a streak of flashing green as she surged away from the seat. 'You know how much I love you. You know. I've surrendered completely to you. You just want me to beg.'

'Of course I want you to beg.' Sam laughed. He couldn't help himself. He went to her and hugged her to him, holding her hard. 'Of course I want you to beg,' he said raggedly. 'I've been begging you for months. It's your turn.'

She struggled away from him furiously, her eyes blazing. 'Sam Wheatley, I have just made a public idiot of myself for you! And, despite your willingness to beat up Martin again, I will probably get the sack because of begging you!'

'I didn't beat him up,' Sam said lazily.

'Sam!' she wailed. 'Be fair! How much harder can I possibly, possibly beg? What can I do to convince you how much I love you?'

'You could have sex with me,' he said evenly.

'Oh, I don't think so, Sam.' Laughing at that, she danced away from his seeking hands. 'Oh, no, that's going too far. I'm sorry. It's been too long. I'm off sex. I'm hooked on celibacy now.'

'I can see I'm just going to have to unhook you.' Moving fast, he reached her before she could get away. Ignoring her shrieks, he lifted her over his shoulder, fireman-style, and carried her off towards the flat. 'This may take some time,' he said mock-wearily. 'It's time I convinced you that we're going to stay happily married for the rest of our lives.'

'I'm going to take some convincing,' she said breathlessly. 'A lot of convincing. A huge, long, incredible lot of convincing.'

'Will's covering me this afternoon so we've got about eighteen hours for a start.' He unlocked the front door, carried her inside and tumbled her onto the bed. 'And then sixty or seventy years after that. Martin's going to have to cover your work for the rest of the day.'

'Work?' Cathie laughed, kissing him and rubbing her face against him as they struggled urgently out of their clothes. '*Work?* What's that?'

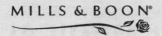

MILLS & BOON®

Makes any time special

Enjoy a romantic novel from
Mills & Boon®

Presents...™   *Enchanted*™   TEMPTATION.

Historical Romance™   ◢ **MEDICAL**
ROMANCE™

MAT1

FREE!

4 Books
and a surprise gift!

We would like to take this opportunity to thank you for reading this Mills & Boon® book by offering you the chance to take FOUR more specially selected titles from the Medical Romance™ series absolutely FREE! We're also making this offer to introduce you to the benefits of the Reader Service™—

  ★ FREE home delivery
  ★ FREE gifts and competitions
  ★ FREE monthly Newsletter
  ★ Books available before they're in the shops
  ★ Exclusive Reader Service discounts

Accepting these FREE books and gift places you under no obligation to buy; you may cancel at any time, even after receiving your free shipment. Simply complete your details below and return the entire page to the address below. *You don't even need a stamp!*

YES! Please send me 4 free Medical Romance books and a surprise gift. I understand that unless you hear from me, I will receive 6 superb new titles every month for just £2.40 each, postage and packing free. I am under no obligation to purchase any books and may cancel my subscription at any time. The free books and gift will be mine to keep in any case.

MOEB

Ms/Mrs/Miss/Mr ....Initials.................................
BLOCK CAPITALS PLEASE

Surname...

Address...

....

....Postcode ....

Send this whole page to:
UK: The Reader Service, FREEPOST CN81, Croydon, CR9 3WZ
EIRE: The Reader Service, PO Box 4546, Kilcock, County Kildare (stamp required)

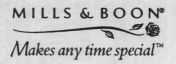